WIDE-OPEN PLANET

By
L. SPRAGUE DE CAMP

I0616966

ARMCHAIR FICTION
PO Box 4369, Medford, Oregon   97501-0168

AN INTERPLANETARY CON MAN

When Felix Borel landed on the planet Krishna, it was with one thought only—to pull off the biggest scam of his long career as a planet-hopping con artist. This time he had set his sights on the treasury of the Republic of Mikardand—a backwards, often violent kingdom that held lots and lots of gold in its treasury. After gaining a hero's status with his lucky slaying of a notorious river pirate, it seemed that pulling off his scheme was going to be almost too easy. Indeed, Borel had the local higher-ups eating out of his hand, seemingly ready to give him nearly anything he wanted. But then Felix Borel met the Lady Zerdai, a gorgeous Krishnan female, who fell head-over-heels in love with the conniving Earthman. Unfortunately for Borel, her affections soon landed him in an arena facing a well-armed foe intent on slitting his throat!

FOR A COMPLETE SECOND NOVEL, TURN TO PAGE 75

CAST OF CHARACTERS

FELIX BOREL
A wily con man if there ever was one. Yet in spite of his many faults he was something of a lovable rogue.

LADY ZERDAI
For a creature with antennae, she was damned good-looking, but her heart belonged to a man from Earth.

YEREVATS
He wasn't the prettiest creature on the planet, but he proved to be a loyal guide and companion for his master.

KUBANAN
As head of the kingdom treasury, all matters of money needed his approval, which he seemed to give almost too easily at times.

DJUVAIN
As a Grand Master on the planet of Krishna he held great power, but even he was vulnerable to the scams of a seasoned con man

SURGEZ
He'd been out of town for a long time, but now that he was back he wanted just one thing—Felix Borel's head on a platter!

CHAPTER ONE

"MY GOOD Senhor," said Abreu, "where the devil did you get those? Raid half the Earth's pawnshops?" He bent closer to look at the decorations on Felix Borel's chest. "Teutonic Order, French Legion of Honor, Third World War, Public Service Award of North America, Fourth Degree of the Knights of St. Stephen, Danish Order of the Elephant, something-or-other from Japan, Intercollegiate Basketball Championship, Pistol Championship of the Policia do Rio de Janeiro... *Tamates,* what a collection!"

Borel smiled sardonically down on the fat little security officer. "You never can tell. I might be a basketball champion." "What are you going to do, sell these things to the poor ignorant Krishnans?"

"I might, if I ran short. Or maybe I'll just dazzle them so they'll give me whatever I ask for."

"Humph. I admit that in that private uniform, with all those medals and orders, you're an awe-inspiring spectacle."

Borel, amusedly watching Abreu fume, knew that the latter was sore because he had not been able to find any excuse to hold Borel at Novorecife. *Thank God,* thought Borel, *the universe is not yet so carefully organized that personal influence can't perform a trick or two.* He would have liked to do Abreu a bad turn if for no better reason than that he harbored an irrational prejudice against Brazzies, as though it were Abreu's fault that his native country was the Earth's leading power.

Borel grinned at the bureaucrat.

"You'd be surprised how helpful this—uh—costume of mine has been. Flunkeys at spaceports assume I'm at least Chief of Staff of the World Federation. 'Step this way, Senhor! Come to the head of the line, Senhor!' More fun than a circus."

Abreu sighed. "Well, I can't stop you. I still think you'd have a better chance of survival disguised as a Krishnan, though."

"And wear a green wig, and false feelers on my forehead? No thanks."

"That's your funeral. However, remember Regulation 368 of the Interplanetary Council rules. You know it?"

"Sure. *'It is forbidden to communicate to any native resident of the planet Krishna any device, appliance, machine, tool, weapon, or invention representing an improvement upon the science and techniques already in existence upon this planet...'* Want me to go on?"

"Nao, you know it. Remember that while the *Viagens Interplanetarias* will ordinarily let you alone once you leave Novorecife, we'll go to any length to prevent and punish any violation of that rule. That's Council orders."

Borel yawned. "I understand. If the type has finished X-raying my baggage, I'll be pushing off. What's the best route to Mishe at present?"

"You could go straight through the Koloft Swamps, but the wilder tribes of the Koloftuma sometimes kill travelers for their goods. You'd better take a raft down the Pichide to Quo, and follow the road southwest from there to Mishe."

"*Obrigado.* The Republic of Mikardand is on a gold standard, isn't it?"

"*Pois sim.*"

"And what's gold at Novorecife worth in terms of World Federation dollars on Earth?"

"Oh, *Deus meu!* That takes a higher mathematician to calculate, what with freight and interest and the balance of trade."

"Just approximately," persisted Borel.

"As I remember, a little less than two dollars a gram."

Borel stood up and shook back his red hair with a characteristic gesture. He gathered up his papers. *"Adeus,* Senhor Cristovao; you've been most helpful."

He smiled broadly as he said this, for Abreu had obviously wanted to be anything but helpful and was still gently simmering over his failure to halt Borel's invasion of Krishna.

THE NEXT DAY found Felix Borel drifting down the Pichide on a timber-raft under the tall clouds that paraded across the greenish sky of Krishna. Next to him crouched the Kolofty servant he had hired at Novorecife, tailed and monstrously ugly.

A brisk shower had just ended.

Borel stood up and shook drops off his cloak as the big yellow sun struck them. Yerevats did likewise, grumbling in broken Gozashtandou: "If master do like I say, put on poor man clothes, could take towboat and stay close to shore. Then when rain come, could put up tarpaulin. No get wet, no be afraid robbers."

"That's my responsibility," replied Borel, moving about to get his circulation going again. He gazed off to starboard, where the low shore of the Pichide broke up into a swarm of reedy islets. "What's that?" he asked, pointing.

"Koloft Swamps," said Yerevats.

"Your people live there?"

"No, not by river. Further back. By river is all *ujero.*" (He gave the Koloftou name for the quasi-human people of the planet, whom most Earthmen thought of simply as Krishans because they were the dominant species.) "Robbers," he added.

Borel, looking at the dark horizontal stripe of reeds between sky and water, wondered if he'd been wise to reject Yerevats's advice to buy the full panoply of a *garm* or knight. Yerevats, he suspected had been hoping for a fancy suit of armor for himself. Borel had turned down the idea on grounds of expense and weight; suppose one fell into the Pichide in all that stove piping? Also, he now admitted to himself, he had succumbed to Earthly prejudice against medieval Krishman weapons, since one Earthly bomb could easily wipe out a whole Krishnan city and one gun mow down a whole army. Perhaps he hadn't given enough weight to the fact that where he was going, no Earthly bombs or guns would be available.

Too late now for might-have-beens, Borel checked over the armament he had finally bought: a sword for himself, as much a badge of status as a protection. A cheap mace with a wooden handle and a star-shaped iron head for Yerevats. Sheath knives of general utility for both. Finally, a crossbow. Privately Borel, no swashbuckler, hoped that any fighting they did would be at as long a range as possible. He had tried drawing a longbow in the Outfitting Shop at Novorecife, but in his unskilled grip it bobbled about too much, and would have required more practice than he had time for.

Borel folded his cloak, laid it on his barracks bag, and sat down to go over his plans again. The only flaw he could see lay in the matter of getting an entree to the Order of Qarar after he arrived at Mishe. Once he'd made friends with members of the Brotherhood, the rest should be easy. By all accounts the Mikardanduma were natural-born suckers. But how to take that first step? He'd probably have to improvise after he got there.

Once he'd gotten over that first hurdle, his careful preparation and experience in rackets like this would see him through. And the best part would be that he'd have the laugh on old Abreu, who could do absolutely nothing about it. Since Borel considered honesty a sign of stupidity, and since Abreu was not stupid for all his pompous ways, Borel assumed that Abreu must be out for what he could get like other wise joes, and that his moral attitudes and talk of principles were mere hypocritical pretence.

"*Ao!*" The shout of one of the raftmen broke into Borel's reverie. The Krishnan was pointing off towards the right bank, where a boat was emerging from among the islets.

Yerevats jumped, up, shading his eyes with his hairy hand. "Robbers!" he said.

"How can you tell from here?" asked Borel, a horrid fear making his heart pound.

"Just know. You see," said the Koloftu, his tail twitching nervously. He looked appealingly at Borel. "Brave master kill robbers? No let them hurt us?"

"Sh-sure," said Borel. He pulled out his sword halfway, looked at the blade, and shoved it back into its scabbard, more as a nervous gesture than anything else.

"*Ohe!*" said one of the raftmen. "Think you to fight the robbers?"

"I suppose so," said Borel.

"No, you shall not! If we make no fight, they will slay only you, for we are but poor men."

"Is that so?" said Borel. The adrenaline being poured into his system made him contrary, and his voice rose. "So you think I'll let my throat be cut quietly to save yours, huh? I'll show you *baghana!*" The sword whipped out of the scabbard, and the flat slapped the raftman on the side of the head, staggering him. "We'll fight whether you like it or not! I'll kill the first coward myself!" He was screaming at the three raftmen, now huddled together fearfully. "Make a barricade of the baggage! Move that stove forward!" He stood over them, shouting and swishing the air with his sword, until they had arranged the movables in a rough square.

"Now," said Borel more calmly, "bring your poles and crouch down inside there. You too, Yerevats. I'll try to hold them off with the bow. If they board us anyway, we'll jump out and rush them when I give the signal. Understand?"

THE BOAT had been slanting out from the shore on a course converging toward that of the raft. Now Borel, peering over the edge of his barricade, could make out the individuals in it. There was one in the bow, another in the stern, and the rest rowing—perhaps twenty in all.

"Is time to cock bow," muttered Yerevats.

The others looked nervously over their shoulders as if wondering whether the river offered a better chance of safety than battle.

Borel said: "I wouldn't try to swim ashore. You know the monsters of the Pichide." Which only made them look unhappier.

Borel put his foot into the stirrup at the muzzle end of the crossbow and cocked the device with both hands and a grunt. Then he opened the bandoleer he had bought with the bow and took out one of the bolts—an iron rod a span long, with a notch at one end, and at the other a flattened, diamond-shaped head with a twist to make the missile spin in its flight. He inserted the bolt into its groove.

The boat came closer and closer. The man in the front end called across the water: "Surrender!"

"Keep quiet," said Borel softly to his companions. By now he was so keyed up that he was almost enjoying the excitement.

Again the man in the boat hailed: "Surrender and we'll not hurt you! 'Tis only your goods we want!"

Still no reply from the raft.

"For the last time, give up, or we'll torture you all to death!"

Borel shifted the crossbow to cover the man in the front. Damn, why hadn't these gloops put sights on their gadgets? He'd taken a few practice shots at a piece of paper the day before and thought himself pretty good. Now, however, his target seemed to shrink to mosquito size every time he tried to draw a bead on it, and something must be shaking the raft to make the weapon waver so.

The man in the bow of the boat had produced an object like a small anchor with extra flukes, tied to the end of a rope. He held this dangling while the grunting oarsmen brought the boat swiftly towards the raft, then whirled it around his head.

Borel shut his eyes and jerked the trigger. The string snapped loudly and the stick kicked back against his shoulder. One of the raftmen whooped.

When Borel opened his eyes, the man in the front of the boat was no longer whirling the grapnel. Instead he was looking back towards the stern, where the man who had sat at the tiller had slumped down. The rowers were resting on their oars and jabbering excitedly.

"Great master hit robber captain!" said Yerevats. "Better cock bow again."

Borel stood up to do so. Evidently he had missed the man he aimed at and instead hit the man in the stern. However, he said nothing to disillusion his servant about his marksmanship.

The boat had reorganized and was coming on again, another robber having taken the place of the one at the tiller. This time there were two Krishnans in front, one with the grapnel and the other with a longbow.

"Keep your heads down," said Borel, and shot at the archer; the bolt flew far over the man's head. Borel started to get up to reload, then realized that he'd be making a fine target. Could you cock these damned things sitting down? The archer let fly his shaft, which passed Borel's head with a frightening *whisht*. Borel hastily found that he could cock his crossbow in a sitting position; albeit a little awkwardly. Another arrow thudded into the baggage.

BOREL SHED his military-style cap as too tempting a target and sighted on the boat again. Another miss, and the boat came closer. The archer was letting off three arrows to everyone of Borel's bolts, though Borel surmised that he was doing so to cover their approach rather than with hope of hitting anybody.

Borel shot again; this time the bolt banged into the planking of the boat. The man with the grapnel was whirling it once more, and another arrow screeched past.

"Hey," said Borel to one of the raftmen, "you with the hatchet! When the grapnel comes aboard, jump out and cut the rope. You other two, get ready to push the boat off with your poles."

"But the arrows—" bleated the first man spoken to.

"I'll take care of that," said Borel with more confidence than he felt.

The archer had drawn another arrow but was holding it steady instead of releasing it. As the boat came within range of the grapnel, the man whirling it let go. It landed on the raft with a thump. Then the man who had thrown it began to pull it in hand over hand until one of the flukes caught in a log.

Borel looked around frantically for some way of the tempting the archer to shoot, since otherwise the first to stand up on the raft would be a sitting duck. He seized his cap and raised it above the edge of the barricade. Snap! and another arrow hissed by.

"Go to it!" shrieked Borel, and sighted on the archer. His crew hesitated. The archer reached back to his quiver for another arrow, and Borel, forcing himself to be calm, drew a bead on the man's body and squeezed.

The man gave a loud animal cry, between a grunt and a scream, and doubled over.

"Go on!" yelled Borel again, raising the crossbow as if to beat the raftmen over the head with it. They sprang into life; one severed the rope with a chop of his hatchet while the other two poked at the boat with their poles.

The remaining man in the front of the boat dropped his rope, shouted something to the rowers, and bent to pick up a boat hook. Borel shot at him, but let himself get excited and missed, though it was practically spitting-distance. When the boat-hook caught in the logs, the man hauled the bow of the boat closer, while a few of the forward rowers stopped rowing to cluster around him with weapons ready.

In desperation Borel dropped his crossbow, grabbed the end of the boat hook, wrenched it out of the wood, and jerked it towards himself. The man on the other end held on a second too long and toppled into the water, still gripping the shaft. Borel pulled on it with some idea of wrenching at away and reversing it to spear the man in the water. However, the latter held on and was hauled to the edge of the raft, where he made as though to climb aboard. Meanwhile the raftmen had again pushed the boat away with their poles, so that those who had been gathering themselves to jump across thought better of the idea.

Thump! Yerevats brought his mace down on the head of the man in the water, and the mop of green hair sank beneath the surface.

The raftmen were now yelling triumphantly in their own dialect. A robber, however, had picked up the longbow from the bottom of the boat and was fumbling with an arrow. Borel, recovering his crossbow, took pains with his next shot and made a hit just as the new archer let fly. The arrow went wild and the archer disappeared, to bob up again a second later cursing and holding his shoulder.

Borel cocked his crossbow again and aimed at the man in the boat. This time, however, instead of shooting, he simply pointed it at one man after another. Each man in turn tried to duck down behind the thwarts, so that organized rowing became impossible.

"Had enough?" called Borel.

The robbers were arguing again, until finally one called out: "All right, don't shoot; we'll let you go." The oars resumed their regular rhythm, and the boat swung away towards the swamp. When it was safely out of range some of the robbers yelled back threats and insults, which Borel could not understand at the distance.

The raftmen were slapping each other's backs, shouting: "We're good! Said I not we could lick a hundred robbers?" Yerevats babbled about his wonderful master.

Borel felt suddenly weak and shaky. If a mouse, or whatever they had on Krishna that corresponded to a mouse, were to climb aboard and squeak at him, he was sure he'd leap into the muddy Pichide in sheer terror. However, it wouldn't do to show that. With trembling hands he inserted a cigarette into his long jeweled holder and lit it. Then he said: "Yerevats, my damned boots seem to have gotten scuffed. Give them a shine, will you?"

CHAPTER TWO

THEY TIED up at Qoa that evening to spend the night. Felix Borel paid off the raftmen, whom he overheard before he retired telling the innkeeper how they had (with some help from the Earthman) beaten off a hundred river-pirates and slain scores. Next morning he bade them goodbye as they pushed off down the river for Madjbur at the mouth of the Pichide, where they meant to sell their logs and catch a towboat back home.

Four long Krishnan days later Borel was pacing the roof of his inn in Mishe. The capitol of the Republic of Mikardand had proved a bigger city than he had expected. In the middle rose a sharp-edged mesa-like hill surmounted by the great citadel of the Order of Qarar. The citadel frowned down upon Borel, who frowned right back as he cast and rejected one plan after another for penetrating not only the citadel but also the ruling caste whose stronghold it was.

He called: "Yerevats!"

"Yes, master?"

"The *Garma Qararuma* toil not, neither do they spin, do they?"

"Guardians work? No sir! Run country, protect common people from enemies and from each other. That enough, not?"

"Maybe, but that's not what I'm after. How are these Guardians supported?"

"Collect taxes from common people."

"I thought so. Who collects these taxes?"

"Squires of Order. Work for treasurer of Order."

"Who's he?" asked Borel.

"Is most noble *garm* Kubanan."

"Where could I find the most noble Sir Kubanan?"

"If he in citadel, no can see. If in treasury office, can."

"Where's the treasury office?"

Yerevats waved vaguely. "That way. Master want go?"

"Right. Get out the buggy, will you?"

Yerevats disappeared, and presently they were rattling over the cobblestone towards the treasury office in the light one-aya four-wheeled carriage Borel had bought in Qou. It had occurred to him at the time that one pictured a gallant knight as pricking o'er the plain on his foaming steed rather than sitting comfortably behind the steed in a buggy. However, since the latter procedure promised to be pleasanter, and Yerevats knew how to drive, Borel had taken a chance on the Mikardanders' prejudices.

The treasury office was in one of the big graceless rough-stone buildings that the Qararuma used as their official architectural style. The doorway was flanked by a pair of rampant stone yekis, the dominant carnivores of this part of the planet, something like a six-legged mink blown up to tiger-size. Borel had had the wits scared out of him by hearing the roar of one on his drive down from Qou.

Borel gathered up his sword, got down from the buggy, assumed his loftiest expression, and asked the doorman: "Where do I find the receiver of taxes, my good man?"

In accordance with the doorman's directions he followed a hall in the building until he discovered a window in the side of the hall, behind which sat a man in the drab dress of the commoners of Mikardand.

Borel said: "I wish to see whether I owe the Republic any taxes. I don't wish to discuss it with you, though; fetch your superior."

The clerk scuttled off with a look compounded of fright and resentment. Presently another face and torso appeared at the window. The torso was clad in the gay coat of a member of the Order of Qarar, but judging from the smallness of the dragon-like emblem on the chest, the man was only a squire or whatever you'd call the grade below the true *garma*.

"Oh, not you," said Borel. "The head of the department."

The squire frowned so that the antennae sprouting from between his brows crossed. "Who are you, anyhow?" he said. "The receiver of taxes am I. If you have anything to pay—"

"My dear fellow," said Borel, "I'm not criticizing you, but as a past Grand Master of an Earthly Order and a member of several others, I'm not accustomed to dealing with underlings. You will kindly tell the head of your department that the *garm* Felix Borel is here."

THE MAN went off shaking his head in a baffled manner. Presently another man with a knight's insignia stepped through a door into the corridor and advanced with hand outstretched.

"My dear sir!" he said. "Will you step into my chamber? 'Tis a pleasure extraordinary to meet a true knight from Earth. I knew not that such lived there; the *Ertsuma* who have come to Mikardand speak strange subversive doctrines of liberty and equality for the commonality—

even those who claim the rank, like that Sir Erik Koskelainen. One can tell you're a man of true quality."

"Thank you," said Borel. "I knew that one of the *Garma Qararuma* would know me as spiritually one of themselves, even though I belong to another race."

The knight bowed. "And now what's this about your wishing to pay taxes? When I first heard it I believed it not; in all the history of the Republic no man has ever offered to pay taxes of his own will."

Borel smiled. "I didn't say I actually *wanted* to pay them. But I'm new here and wanted to know my rights and obligations. That's all. Better to get them straightened out at the start, don't you think?"

"Yes—but—are you he who came hither from Qou but now?"

"Yes."

"He who slew Ushyarian the river-pirate and his lieutenant in battle on the Pichide?"

Borel waved a deprecating hand. "That was nothing. One can't let such rogues run loose, you know. I'd have wiped out the lot, but one can't chase malefactors with a timber-raft."

The Qararu jumped up. "Then the reward is due you!"

"Reward?"

"Why, knew you not? A reward of ten thousand *karda* has lain on the head of Ushyarian for years! I must see about the verification of your claim…"

Borel, thinking quickly, said:

"Don't bother. I don't really want it."

"You don't wish it?" The man stared blankly.

"No. I only did a gentleman's duty, and I don't need it."

"But—the money's here—it's been appropriated—"

"Well, give it to some worthy cause. Don't you have charities in Mishe?"

The knight finally pulled himself together. "Extraordinary. You must meet the treasurer himself. As for taxes—let me see—there is a residence tax on metics, while on the other hand we have treaties with Gozashtand and some of the other states to exempt each other's gentle-folk. I know not how that would affect you—but concern yourself not in view of your action in the matter of the reward. I'll put it up to the treasurer. Can you wait?"

"Sure. Mind if I smoke?"

"Not at all. Have one of these." The knight dug a bunch of Krishnan cigars out of a desk drawer.

AFTER A few minutes, the official returned and asked Borel to come to the treasurer's office, where he introduced the Earthman to the treasurer of the Order. Sir Kubanan was that rarity among Krishnans, a stout man, looking a little like a beardless Santa Claus.

The previous conversation more or less repeated itself, except that the treasurer proved a garrulous old party with a tendency to ramble. He seemed fascinated by Borel's medals.

"This?" said Borel, indicating the basketball medal. "Oh, that's the second degree of the Secret Order of Spooks. Very secret and very powerful; only admits men who've been acquitted of a murder charge…"

"'Wonderful, wonderful," said Kubanan at last. "My dear sir, we will find a way around this tax matter, fear not. Perish the thought that one so chivalrous as yourself should be taxed like a vulgar commoner, even though the Order be sore pressed for funds."

This was the opening Borel had been waiting for. He pounced. "The Order would like additional sources of revenue?"

"Why, yes. Of course we're all sworn to poverty and obedience." (he contemplated his glittering assortment of rings) "and hold all in common, even our women and children. Nevertheless, the defense of the Republic puts a heavy burden upon us."

"Have you thought of a state lottery?"

"What might that be?"

Borel explained, rattling through the details as fast as his fair command of the language allowed.

"Wonderful," said Kubanan. "I fear I could not follow your description at all times, though; you do speak with an accent. Could you put it in writing for us?"

"Sure. In fact I can do better than that."

"How mean you?"

"Well, to give you an example, it's much easier to tell how to ride an aya than to do it, isn't it?"

"Yes."

"Just so, it's easy to tell you how a lottery works—but it takes practical experience to run one."

"How can we surmount that difficulty?"

"I could organize and run your first lottery."

"Sir Felix, you quite take my breath away. Could you write down the amounts involved in this scheme?"

Borel wrote down a rough estimate of the sums he might expect to take in and pay out in a city of this size. Kubanan, frowning, said: "What's this ten percent for the Director?"

"That's the incentive. If you're going to run this thing in a businesslike manner after I've left, we'd better set it up right. And one must have an incentive. The first time I'd be the director, naturally."

"I see. That's not unreasonable. But since members of the Order aren't allowed private funds beyond mere pocket-money, how would the commission act as incentive?"

Borel shrugged. "You'd have to figure that one out. Maybe you'd better hire a commoner to run the show. I suppose there are merchants and bankers among them, aren't there?"

"True. Amazing. We must discuss this further. Won't you come to my chambers this evening to sup? I'll pass you in to the citadel."

Borel tried to hide his grin of triumph as he said: "It's my turn to be overwhelmed, your Excellency!" The Borel luck!

AT THE appointed hour Borel, having presented his pass at the gate of the citadel, was taken in tow by a uniformed guide. Inside Mishe's Kremlin stood a lot of huge plain stone buildings wherein the Guardians led their ant-like existence. Borel walked past playgrounds and exercise-grounds, and identified other buildings as apartment houses, armories, office-buildings, and an auditorium. It was just as well to memorize such details in case a slipup should require a hasty retreat. Borel had once spent six months as a guest of the French Republic in consequence of failing to observe this precaution. He passed hundreds of gorgeously arrayed *garma* of both sexes. Some looked at him sharply, but none offered interference.

For the quarters of one sworn to poverty, the treasurer's apartment was certainly sumptuous. Kubanan cordially introduced Borel to a young female Mikardandu who quite took his breath away. If one didn't mind green hair, feathery antennae, and a somewhat flat-featured Oriental look, she was easily the most beautiful thing he'd seen since Earth, especially since the Mikardandu evening dress began at the midriff.

"Sir Felix, my confidential secretary, the Lady Zerdai." Kubanan lowered his voice in mock confidence. "I *think* she's my own daughter, though naturally one can never know for sure."

"Then family feeling does exist among the Guardians?" said Borel.

"Yes, I fear me it does. A shameful weakness, but nevertheless a most pleasant one. Heigh-ho, at times I envy the commoners. Why, Zerdai herself has somehow bribed the women in charge of the incubator to show her which is her own authentic egg."

Zerdai sparkled at them. "I was down there but today, and the maids tell me it's due to hatch in another fifteen days!"

"Ahem," said Borel. "Would it be good manners to ask who's papa? Excuse me if I pull a boner occasionally; I'm not entirely oriented yet."

Kubanan said: "No offense, sir. He was Sir Sardu, the predecessor of Sir Shurgez, was he not, Zerdai?"

"Yes," she agreed. "But our petty affairs must seem dull to a galaxy-traveler like you, Six Felix. Tell us of the Earth! I've long dreamed of going thither; I can fancy nought more glamorous than seeing the New York Stock Exchange, or the Moscow Art Theater, or the Shanghai nightclubs with my own eyes. It must be wonderful to ride in a power-vehicle! To talk to somebody miles distant! And all those marvelous inventions and factories…"

Kubanan said dryly: "I sometimes think Lady Zerdai shows an unbecoming lack of pride in her Order, young though she be. Now about this lottery: will you see to having the certificates printed?"

"Certainly," said Borel. "So you do have a printing-press here?"

"Yes; from the Earthmen we got it. We'd have preferred a few Earthly weapons to smite our enemies; but no, all they'll let us have is this device, which bodes ill for our social order. Should the commoners learn reading, who knows what mad ideas this ill-starred machine may spread among them?"

BOREL TURNED on the charm, thankful that supper consisted of some of the more palatable Krishnan dishes. On this planet you were liable to have something like a giant cockroach set before you as a treat. Afterwards all three lit cigars and talked while sipping a liqueur.

Kubanan continued: "Sir Felix, you're old enough in the ways of the world to know that a man's pretext is often other than his true reason. Your Earthmen tell me they hide their sciences from us because our culture is yet too immature—by which they mean our gladiatorial shows, our trials by combat, our warring national sovereignties, our social inequalities, and the like. Now, I say not that they're altogether wrong—I for one should be glad had they never introduced this accursed printing press. But the question I'd ask you is: What's their real reason?"

Borel wrinkled his forehead in the effort of composing a suitable reply. Being an adventurer and no intellectual he'd never troubled his head much about such abstract questions. At last, he said: "Perhaps they're afraid the

Krishnans, with their warlike traditions, would learn to make spaceships and attack their neighboring planets."

"A fantastic idea," said Kubanan. "'Tis not so long since there was a tremendous uproar over the question of whether the planets were inhabited. The churches had been assuring us that the planets were the very gods, and crucifying heretics who said otherwise. No wonder we hailed as gods the first beings from Earth and the other planets of your sun!"

Borel murmured a polite assent, privately thinking that the first expedition to this system ought, if they had any sense, to have been satisfied with being gods and not go disillusioning the Krishnans. That's what came of letting a bunch of sappy do-gooders...

Kubanan was going on: "Our problem is much more immediate. We're hemmed and beset by enemies. Across the Pichide lies Gozashtand, whose ruler has been taking an unfriendly line of late; and Madjbur City is a veritable hotbed of plots and stratagems. If a way could be found to get us—let's say—one gun, which our clever smiths could copy, there's nothing the Order would not do..."

So, thought Borel, *that's why the old boy is so hospitable to a mere stranger.* He said: "I see your point, Excellency. You know the risks, don't you?"

"The greater the risk, the greater the reward."

"True, but it would require most careful thought. I'll let you know when I've had time to think."

"I understand." Kubanan rose, and to Borel's surprise said: "I leave you now; Kuri will think I've forgotten her utterly. You'll stay the night, of course?"

"Why, I—thank you, your Excellency. I'll have to send a note out to my man."

"Yes, yes, I'll send you a page. Meanwhile the Lady Zerdai shall keep you company, or if you've a mind to read there are ample books on the shelves. Take the second room on the left."

BOREL murmured his thanks and the treasurer departed, his furred robe floating behind him. Then, having no interest whatever in Kubanan's library, he sat down near Zerdai.

Eyes aglow, Zerdai said: "Now that we need talk finance no more, tell me of the Earth. How live you? I mean, what's your system of personal relationships? Have you homes and families like the commoners, or all in common as we Guardians do?"

As Borel explained, the girl sighed. With a far-away look she said: "Could I but go thither! I can imagine nought more romantic than to be an Earthly housewife with a home and a man and children of my own! And a telephone!"

Borel reflected that some Earthly housewives sang a different tune, but said gently: "Couldn't you resign from the Order?"

"In theory, yes—but 'tis hardly ever done. 'Twould be like stepping into another world, and what sort of welcome would the commoners give? Would they not resent what they'd call one's airs? And to have to face the scorn of all Guardians... No, it would not do. Could one escape this world entire, as by journeying to Earth..."

"Maybe that could be arranged too," said Borel cautiously. While he was willing to promise her anything to enlist her cooperation and then ditch her, he didn't want to get involved in more schemes at once than he could handle.

"Really?" she said, glowing at him. "There's nought I wouldn't do…"

Borel thought, *they all say there's nothing they wouldn't do if I'll only get them what they want.* He said: "I may need help on some of my projects here. Can I count on your assistance?"

"With all my heart!"

"Good. I'll see that you don't regret it. We'd make a wonderful team, don't you think? With your beauty and my experience there's nothing we couldn't get away with. Can't you see us cutting a swath through the galaxy?"

She leaned toward him, breathing hard. "You're wonderful!"

He smiled. "Not really. You are."

"No, you."

"No, you. You've got beauty, brains, nerve— Oh well, I'll have plenty of chance to tell you in the future. When I get this lottery organized."

"Oh." This seemed to bring her back to Krishna again. She glanced at the time-candle and put out her cigar, saying: "Great stars, I had no idea the hour was so late! I must go to bed, Sir Felix the Red. Will you escort me to my room?"

CHAPTER THREE

AT BREAKFAST Sir Kubanan said: "Thanks to the stars the Grand Council meets this forenoon. I'll bring up your lottery suggestion, and if they approve we can start work on it today. Why spend you not the morning laying your plans?"

"A splendid idea, Excellency," said Borel, and went to work after breakfast on the design of lottery tickets and advertising posters. Zerdai hung around, asking if she couldn't help, trying to cuddle up beside him and getting in the way of his pen arm, all the time looking at him with such open adoration that even he, normally as unembarrassable as a rhinoceros, squirmed a little under her gaze.

However, he put up with it in a good cause, to wit: the cause of making a killing for Felix E. Borel.

By the middle of the day Kubanan was back jubilant. "They approved! At first Grand Master Djuvain boggled a little, but I talked him round. He liked not letting one not of our Order so deep into our affairs; saying, how can there be a secret Order if all its secrets be known? But I bridled him. How goes the plan?"

Borel showed him the layouts. The treasurer said: "Wonderful! Wonderful! Carry on, my boy, and come to me for aught you need."

"I will. This afternoon I'll arrange for printing this stuff. Then we'll need a booth. How about setting it up at the lower end of that little street up to the gate of the citadel. And I'll have to train a couple of men as ticket-sellers, and some more to guard the money."

"All shall be done. Hearken, why move you not hither from your present lodgings? I have ample room, and 'twould save time as well as augment comfort, thus slaying two unhas with one bolt."

"Do come," sighed Zerdai.

"Okay. Where can I stable my aya and quarter my servant?"

Kubanan told him. The afternoon he spent making arrangements for printing. Since Mishe had but two printers, each with one little hand press, the job would not be finished for at least twenty days.

HE REPORTED this to Kubanan at supper, adding: "Will you give me a draft on the treasury of the Order for fifteen hundred karda to cover the initial costs?" (This was more than fifty percent over the prices the printers had quoted, but Kubanan assented without question.)

"And now," continued Borel, "let's take up the other matter. If Zerdai's your confidential secretary, I don't suppose you mind discussing it in front of her."

"Not at all. You've found a way to get around the technological blockade?"

"Well—yes and no. I can assure you it'll do no good for me to go to Novorecife and try to smuggle out a gun or plans for one. They have a machine that looks right through you, and they make you stand in front of it before letting you out."

"Have they no regard for privacy?"

"Not in this matter. Besides, even if one did succeed, they'd send an agent to bring one back dead or alive."

"Of those agents I've heard," said Kubanan with a slight shudder.

"Moreover I'm no engineer—a base-born trade—so I can't carry a set of plans in my head for your people to work from. Guns are too complicated for that."

"What then?"

"I think the only way is to have something they want so badly they'll ease up on the blockade in return for it."

"Yes, but what have we? There's little of ours that they covet. Even gold, they say, is much too heavy to haul billions of miles to Earth with profit, and almost everything we make, they can make more cheaply at home once they know how. I know; I've discussed it with the *Viagens* folk at Novorecife. Knight though I be, my office requires that I interest myself in such base commercial matters."

Borel drew on his cigar and remarked: "Earthmen are an inventive lot, and they'll continue thinking up new things for a long time to come."

Kubanan shuddered. "A horrid place must this Earth of yours be. No stability."

"So, if we had an invention far ahead of their latest stuff, they might want the secret badly enough to make a deal. See?"

"How can we? We're not inventive here. No gentleman would lower himself by tinkering with machines while the common people lack the wit."

Borel smiled. "Suppose I had such a secret?"

"That would be different. What is it?"

"It's an idea that was confided to me by a dying old man. Although the Earthmen had scorned him and said his device was against the laws of nature, it worked. I know because he showed me a model."

"But what *is* it?" cried Kubanan.

"It would not only be of vast value to the Earthmen, but also would make Mikardand preeminent among the nations of Krishna."

"Torture us not, Sir Felix!" pleaded Zerdai.

"It's a perpetual-motion machine."

Kubanan asked: "What is that?"

"A machine that runs forever, or at least until it wears out."

KUBANAN frowned and twitched his antennae. "Not sure am I that I understand you. We have water-wheels for operating grain-mills which run until they wear out."

"Not quite what I mean." Borel concentrated on putting a scientific concept into words, a hard thing to do because he neither knew nor cared much about such matters. "I mean, this machine will give out more power than is put into it."

"Wherein lies the advantage of that?"

"Why, Earthmen prize power above all things. Power runs their spaceships and motor vehicles, their communications equipment and factories. Power lights their homes and milks their cows... I forget, you don't know about cows. And where do they get their power? From coal, uranium, and things like that. Minerals. They get some from the sun and the tides, but not enough, and they worry about exhaustion of their minerals. Now, my device takes power from the force of gravity, which is the very fundamental quality of matter." He was striding up and down in his eagerness. "Sooner or later Krishna is bound to have a scientific revolution like that of Earth. Neither you nor the *Viagens Interplanetarias* can hold it off forever. And when—"

"I hope I live not to see it," said Kubanan.

"When it comes, don't you want Mikardand to lead the planet? Of course! No need to give up your social system. In fact, if we organize the thing right, it'll not only secure the rule of the Order in Mikardand, but extend the Order's influence over all Krishna!"

Kubanan was beginning to catch a little of Borel's fire. "How propose you to do that?"

"Ever heard of a corporation?"

"Let me think—is that not some vulgar scheme Earthmen use in trade and manufacture?"

"Yes, but there's more to it than that. There's no limit to what you can do with a corporation. The *Viagens* is a corporation, though all of its stock is owned by governments..." Borel plunged into corporation finance, not neglecting to say: "Of course, the promoter of a corporation gets fifty-one percent of the stock in consideration of his services."

"Who would the promoter he in our case?"

"I, naturally. We can form this corporation to finance the machine. The initial financing can come from the Order itself, and later the members can either hold—"

"Wait, wait. How can the members buy stock when they own no money of their own?"

"Uhh...that's a tough one. I guess the treasury'll have to keep the stock; it can either draw profits from the lease of the machines, or sell the stock at an enormous profit—"

"Sir Felix," said Kubanan, "you make my head to spin. No more, lest my head split like a melon on the chopping block. Enticing though your scheme be, there is one immovable obstacle."

"Yes?"

"The Grand Master and the other officers would never permit—you'll not take offense?—would never permit an outsider such as yourself to acquire such power over the Order. 'Twas all I could do to put over your lottery scheme, and this would be one thing too many, like a second nose on your face."

"All right, think it over," said Borel. "Now suppose you tell me about the Order of Qarar."

Kubanan obliged with an account of the heroic deeds of Qarar, the legendary founder of the Order who had slain assorted giants and monsters. As he talked, Borel reflected on his position. He doubted if the Qararuma would want to take in a being from another planet like himself, and even if they did, the club rules against private property would handicap his style.

He asked: "How do Mikardanders become members? By being—uh—hatched in the official incubator?"

"Not always. Each child from the incubator is tested at various times during its growth. If it fails any test, 'tis let out for adoption by some good commoner family. On the other hand, when membership falls low, we watch the children of commoners and any that show exceptional qualities are admitted to training as wards of the Order." The treasurer went on to tell of the various grades of membership until he got sleepy and took his leave.

* * *

Later Borel asked Zerdai: "Love me?"

"You know I do, my lord!"

"Then I have a job for you."

"Aught you say, dearest master."

"I want one of those honorary memberships."

33

"But Felix, that's for notables like the King of Gozashtand only! I know not what I could accomplish—"

"You make the suggestion to Kubanan, see? And keep needling him until he asks me. He trusts you."

"I will try, my dearest. And I hope Shurgez never returns."

While ordinarily Borel would have investigated this last cryptic remark, at the moment his head was too full of schemes for self-aggrandizement. "Another thing. Who's the most skilled metalworker in Mishe? I want somebody who can make a working model that really works."

"I'll find out for you, my knight."

ZERDAI SENT Borel to one Henjare bad-Qavao the Brazer, a gnomish Mikardandu whom Borel first dazzled with his facade and then swore to secrecy with dreadful sounding oaths of his own invention.

He then presented the craftsman with a rough plan for a wheel with a lot of rods with weights on their ends, pivoted to the circumference so that they had some freedom to swing in the plane of rotation of the wheel. There was also a trip arrangement so that as the wheel rotated, each rod as it approached the top was moved from a position leaning back against a stop on the rim to a straight-out radial position. Hence the thing looked as though at any time the weights on one side stood out farther from the center than those on the other, and therefore would over-balance the latter and cause the wheel to turn indefinitely.

Borel knew just enough about science to realize that the device would not work, though not enough to know why. On the other hand, since these gloops knew even less than he did, there should be no trouble in selling them the idea.

That night Kubanan said: "Sir Felix, a brilliant thought has struck me. Won't you accept an honorary membership in our proud Order? In truth, you'll find it a great advantage while you dwell in Mikardand, or even when you journey elsewhere."

Borel registered surprise. "Me? I'm most humbly grateful, Excellency, but is an outsider like myself worthy of such an honor?" Meanwhile he thought: *good old Zerdai! If I was the marrying kind...* For a moment he wavered in his determination to shake her when she'd served her turn.

"Nonsense, my lad, of course you're worthy. I'd have gone farther and proposed you for full membership, but the Council pointed out that the constitution allows that only to native-born Mikardanders of our own species. As 'tis, honorary membership will provide you with most of the privileges of membership and few of the obligations."

"I'm overcome with happiness."

"Of course there's the little matter of the initiation."

"What?" Borel controlled his face.

"Yes; waive it they would not, since no king are you. It amounts to little; much ceremony and a night's vigil. I'll coach you in the ritual. And you must obtain ceremonial robes; I'll make you a list."

Borel wished he'd hiked the printing charges on the lottery material by another fifty percent.

THE INITIATION proved not only expensive, but an interplanetary bore as well. Brothers in fantastic robes and weird masks stood about muttering a mystic chant at intervals. Borel stood in front of the Grand Master of the Order, a tall Krishnan with a lined face that might have been carved from wood for all the expression it bore. Borel responded to interminable questions; since the language was an archaic dialect of Gozashtandou, he did not really know what he was saying half the time. He was lectured on the Order's glorious past, mighty present, and boundless future, and on his duties to protect and defend his interests. He called down all sorts of elaborate astrological misfortunes on his head should he violate his oaths.

"Now," said the grand master, "art thou ready for the vigil. Therefore I command thee: strip to thy underwear!"

Wondering what he was getting into, Borel did so.

"Come with me," said Grand Master Sir Djuvain.

They led him down stairs and through passages that got progressively narrower, darker, and less pleasant. A couple of the hooded brethren carried lanterns, which soon became necessary in order to see the way. *We must be far below the ground level of the citadel,* thought Borel, stumbling along in his damp socks and feeling most clammy and uncomfortable.

When they seemed to have descended into the very bowels of the Earth, they halted. The grand master said: "Here shalt thou remain the night, O aspirant. Danger will come upon thee, and beware how thou meetest it."

One of the brothers was measuring a long candle. He cut it off at a certain length and fixed it up right to a small shelf in the rough side of the tunnel. Another brother handed Borel a hunting spear with a long, broad head.

Then they left him.

So far he had carried off his act by assuring himself that all this was a lot of bluff and hokum. Nothing serious could be intended. As the brothers' footfalls died away, however, he was no longer so sure. The damned candle seemed to illuminate for a distance of only about a meter in all directions. Fore and aft the tunnel receded into utter blackness.

His hair rose as something rustled. As he whipped the spear into position it scuttled away; some rat-like creature no doubt. Borel started pacing. If that damned dope Abreu had only let him bring his watch! Then he'd at least have a notion of the passage of time. It seemed he'd been pacing for hours, though that was probably an illusion.

BOREL BECAME aware of an odd irregularity in the floor beneath his stockinged feet, and he bent down and explored it with his fingers. Yes, a pair of parallel grooves, two or three centimeters deep, ran lengthwise along the tunnel. He followed them a few steps each way, but stopped when he could no longer see what he was doing. Why should there be two parallel grooves like a track along the floor?

He paced until his legs ached from weariness, then tried sitting on the floor with his back against the wall. When he soon found his eyelids drooping, he scrambled up lest his initiators return to find him asleep. The candle burned slowly down, its flame standing perfectly still for minutes at a stretch and then wavering slightly as some tiny air current brushed it. Still silence and darkness.

The candle would soon be burned down to nothing. What then? Would they expect him to stand here in complete darkness?

A sound made him jump violently. He could not tell what sort of sound it: was; merely a faint noise from down the tunnel. There it came again.

Then his hair really rose at a low throaty vocal noise, the kind one hears in the carnivore cage of the zoo before feeding time. A sort of grunt, such as a big cat makes in tuning up for a real roar. It came again, louder.

The dying candle flame showed to Borel's horrified gaze something moving fast towards him in the tunnel. With a frightful roar a great yeki rushed into the dim light with gleaming eyes and bared fangs.

For perhaps a second (though it seemed an hour) Felix Borel stood helplessly holding his spear poised, his mouth hanging open. In that second, however, his mind suddenly worked with the speed of a tripped mousetrap. Something odd about the yeki's motion, together with the fact of the grooves in the floor, gave him the answer: the animal was a stuffed one pushed towards him on wheels.

Borel bent and laid his spear diagonally across the floor of the tunnel, and stepped back. When the contraption struck the spear it slewed sideways with a bang, rattle, and thump and stopped, its nose against the wall.

Borel recovered his spear and examined the derailed yeki at close range. It proved a pretty battered looking piece of taxidermy, the head and neck criss-crossed with seams where the hide had been slashed open and sewn up again. Evidently it had been used for initiation for a long time, and some of the aspirants had speared it. Others had doubtless turned tail and run, thus flunking the test.

Footsteps sounded in the corridor and lanterns bobbed closer just as the candle on the shelf guttered out. The grand master and the masked brethren swarmed around Borel, including one with a horn on which he had made the yeki-noises. They slapped him on the back and told him how brave he was, then led him back up many flights to the main hall, where he was allowed to don his clothes again. The grand master hung a jeweled dragon insignia around his neck and welcomed him with a florid speech in archaic style:

"O Felix, be thou hereby accepted into this most noble, most ancient, most honorable, most secret, most puissant, most righteous, most chivalrous, and most fraternal Order, and upon thee be bestowed all the rights, privileges, rank, standing, immunities, duties, liabilities, obligations, and attributes of a knight of this most noble, most ancient, most honorable..."

The long Krishnan night was two-thirds gone when the handshaking and drinking were over. Borel and Kubanan, arms about each other's necks, wove their way drunkenly to the latter's apartment while Borel sang what he could remember of an Earthly song about a King of England and a queen of Spain, until Kubanan shushed him, saying:

"Know you not that poetry's forbidden in Midardand?"

"I didn't know. Why?"

"The Order decided it was bad for our—hic—martial spirit. B'sides, poets tell too damned many lies. What's the next stanza?"

CHAPTER FOUR

NEXT MORNING Sir Felix, as he tried to remember to think of himself, began to press for consideration of his perpetual motion scheme. He obtained an interview with Grand Master Djuvain in the afternoon and put his proposal. Sir Djuvain seemed puzzled by the whole thing and Borel had to call in Kubanan to help him explain.

Djuvain finally said: "Very well, Brother Felix, tell me when your preparations are ready and I'll call a general meeting of the members in residence to pass upon your proposal."

Then, since the working model was not yet ready. Borel had nothing to do for a couple of days except breathe down the neck of Henjare the Brazer and superintend the building of the lottery ticket booth. The printing job was nowhere near done.

Therefore he whistled up Yerevats to help him pass the time by practicing driving the buggy. After a couple of hours he could fairly well manage the difficult art of backing and filling to turn around in a restricted space.

"Have the carriage ready right after lunch," he ordered.

"Master go ride?"

"Yes. I shan't need you though; I'm taking it myself."

"Unk. No Good. Master get in trouble."

"That's my lookout."

"Bet master take girl out. Bad business."

"Mind your own business!" shouted Borel, and made a pass at Yerevats, who ducked and scuttled out. Now, thought Borel, *Yerevats, will sulk and I'll have to spend a day cajoling him back into a good humor or I'll get no decent service.* Damn it, why didn't they have mechanical servants with no feelings that their masters had to take into account? Somebody had tried to make one on Earth, but the thing had run amok and mistaken its master for a cord of firewood...

THE AFTERNOON saw him trotting down the main avenue of Mishe with Zerdai by his side looking at him worshipfully. He could not get quite used to the curious sound made by the six hooves of the aya when it trotted.

He asked: "Who has the right of way if somebody comes in from the side ?"

"Why, you do, Felix. You're a member of the Order, even if not a regular Guardian!"

"Oh." Borel, though he had about as little public spirit as a man can have, had been exposed to the democratic institutions of Earth long enough so as to find these class distinctions distasteful. "In other words, because I'm now an honorary knight, I can tear through the town at full gallop hollering '*byant-hao!*' and if anybody gets run over that's too bad?"

"Naturally. What think you? But I forget you're from another world. 'Tis one of your fascinations that beneath your hard adventuresome exterior you're more gentle and considerate than the men of this land."

Borel hid a smile. He'd been called a lot of things before, including thief, swindler, and slimy double-crossing heel, but never gentle and considerate. Maybe that was an example of the relativity the longhaired scientists talked about.

"Where would you like me to drive you?" he asked.

"To Earth!" she said, putting her head on his shoulder. For a moment he was almost tempted to renege on his plan to leave her behind. Then the resolute selfishness that was the adventurer's leading trait came to his rescue, and he reminded himself that on a fast getaway, the less baggage the better. Love 'em and leave 'em. Anyway, wouldn't she be happier if they parted before she learned he was no do-gooder after all?

"Let's to the tournament ground outside the North Gate. Today's the battle betwixt Sir Volhadj and Sir Shusp."

"What's this? I hadn't heard of it."

"Sir Shusp forced a challenge of Sir Volhadj; some quarrel over the love of a lady. Shusp had already slain three knights in affrays of this kind."

Borel said: "If you Guardians are supposed to have everything in common like the communists we used to have on Earth, I don't see what reason a knight has to get jealous. Couldn't they both court her at once?"

"That's not the custom. A maid should dismiss the one before taking another; to do otherwise is in bad taste."

They reached the North Gate and ambled out into the country. Borel asked: "Where does this road go?"

"Know you not? To Koloft and Novorecife."

Beyond the last houses, where the fanned fields began, the tournament grounds lay to the right of the road. It reminded Borel of a North American high school football field: same small wooden grandstands, and tents at the ends where the goalposts should be. In the middle of one stand a section had been built out into a box in which sat the high officers of the Order. Hawkers circulated through the crowd, one crying: "Flowers! Flowers! Buy a flower with the color of your favorite knight! Red for Volhadj, white for Shusp. Flowers!"

The stands were already full of people who, from the predominan color of the flowers in their hats, seemed to favor Shusp. Borel ignored Zerdai's suggestion that he pitch some commoner out of his seat and claim it for himself, and led her to where the late arrivals clustered standing at one end of the field. He was a little annoyed with himself for not having come in time to lay a few bets. This should be much more exciting than the ponies on Earth, and by shaving the odds and betting both ways he might put himself in the enviable position of making a profit on these saps no matter who won.

AS THEY took their places a trumpet blew. Nearby, Borel saw a man in Moorish-looking armor, wearing a spiked helmet with a nose guard and a little skirt of chain mail; he was sitting on a big tough-looking aya, also wearing bits of armor here and there. This Qararu now left his tent to trot down to the middle of the field. From the red touches about his saddle and equipment Borel judged him to be Sir Volhadj. Volhadj, as the challenged party, had his sympathy, in line with his own distaste for violence. Why couldn't the other gloop be a good fellow about his girl friend? Borel had done that sort of thing and found nobody the worse for it.

From the other end of the field came another rider, similarly equipped but decorated in white. The two met at the center of the field, wheeled to face the grand master, and walked their mounts forward until they were as close as they could get to the booth. The grand master made a speech that Borel could not hear, and then the knights wheeled away and trotted back to their respective ends of the field. At the near end Sir Volhadj's squires, or seconds, or whatever they were, handed him up a lance and a smallish round shield.

The trumpet blew again and the antagonists galloped towards each other. Borel winced as they met with a crash in the middle of the field. When Borel opened his eyes again, he saw that the red knight had been knocked out of the saddle and was rolling over and over on the moss. His aya continued on without him while the white knight slowed gradually as he approached Borel's' end of the field, then turned and headed back.

Volhadj had meanwhile gotten up with a visible effort in his weight of iron and clanked over to where his lance lay. He picked it up, and as Shusp bore down on him he planted the butt-end in the ground and lowered the point to the level of the charging aya's chest, where the creature's light armor did not protect it. Borel could not see the spear go in, but he judged that it had when the beast reared, screamed, threw its rider, and collapsed kicking. Borel, who felt strongly about cruelty to animals, thought indignantly that there ought to be an interplanetary S.P.C.A. to stop this sort of thing.

At this point the crowd began to jostle and push with cries of excitement, so Borel had to take his eyes off the fight long enough to clear a space with his elbows for Zerdai. When he looked back again the knights were at it on foot, making a tremendous din, Shusp with a huge two-handed sword, Volhadj with his buckler and a sword of more normal size.

They circled around one another, slashing, thrusting, and parrying, and worked their way slowly down to Borel's end of the field, till he could see the dents in their armor and the trickle of blood running down the chin of Sir Volhadj. By now, both were so winded that the fight was going as slowly as an honest wrestling match, with both making a few swipes and then stopping to pant and glare at each other for a while.

Then in the midst of an exchange of strokes, Sir Volhadj's sword flew up, turning over and over until it came down at Shusp's feet. Sir Shusp instantly put a foot on it and forced Sir Volhadj back with a swing of his crowbar-like blade. Then he picked up the dropped sword and threw it as far away as he could.

Borel asked: "Hey, is he allowed to do that?"

"I know not," said Zerdai. "Though there be few rules, mayhap that's against them."

Shusp now advanced rapidly on Volhadj, who was reduced to a shield battered all out of shape and a dagger. The latter gave ground, parrying the swipes as best he could.

"Why doesn't the fool cut and run?" asked Borel.

Zerdai stared at him. "Know you not that for a knight of the Order the penalty for cowardice is flaying alive?"

At the rate Volhadj was backing towards them he'd soon be treading on the toes of the spectators, who in fact began to spread out nervously. Volhadj was staggering, disheartening Borel, who hated to see his favorite nearing his rope's end.

ON A SUDDEN impulse, Borel drew his own sword and called: "Hey, Volhadj, don't look now but here's something for you!" With that he threw the sword as if it had been a javelin, so that the point stuck into the ground along side of Volhadj. The latter dropped his dagger, snatched up the sword, and tore into Shusp with renewed vigor.

Then Shusp went down with a clang. Volhadj, standing over him, found a gap in his armor around the throat, put the point there, and pushed down on the hilt with both hands. When Borel opened his eyes again, Shusp's legs were giving their last twitch. Cheers and the paying of bets.

Volhadj came back to where Borel stood and said: "Sir Felix the Red, I perceive you succored me but now."

"How d'you know that?"

"By your empty scabbard, friend. Here take your sword with my thanks. I doubt the referee will hold your deed a foul, since the chief complainant will no longer be present to press his case. Call on me for help any time." He shook hands warmly and walked wearily off to his wigwam.

"'Twas a brave deed, Felix," said Zerdai, squeezing his arm as they walked back to the buggy through the departing crowd.

"I don't see that it was anything special," said Borel truthfully.

"Why, had Sir Shusp won, he'd have challenged you!"

"*Gluk!*" said Borel. He hadn't thought of that.

"What is it, my dearest?"

"Something caught in my throat.

Let's get back to dinner ahead of the crowd, huh? Giddap, Galahad!"

However, Zerdai retired after dinner, saying she would not be back for supper; the excitement had given her a headache.

Kubanan said: "'Tis a rare thing, for she's been in better spirits since your arrival than was her wont since Sir Shurgez departed."

"You mean she was grieving for a boyfriend until I came along and cheered her up?" Borel thought, *Kubanan's a nice old wump; too bad he'll have to be the fall guy for the project. But business is business.*

"Yes. Ah, Felix, it's sad you're of another species, so that she'll never lay you an egg! For the Order can use offspring inheriting your qualities. Even I, sentimental old fool that I am, like to think of you as a son-in-law and Zerdai's eggs as my own grandchildren, as though I were some simple commoner with a family."

Borel asked: "What's this about Shurgez? What happened to him?"

"The grand master ordered him on a quest."

"What quest?"

"To fetch the beard of the King of Balhib."

"And what does the Order want with this king's beard? Are you going into the upholstery business?"

Kubanan laughed. "Of course not. The King of Balhib has treated the Order with scorn and contumely of late, and we thought to tech him a lesson."

"And why was Shurgez sent?"

"Because of his foul murder of Brother Sir Zamran."

"Why did he murder Zamran?"

"Surely you know the tale—but I forget, you're still new here. Sir Zamran was he who slew Shurgez's lady."

"I thought Zerdai was Shurgez's girl."

"She was, but afterward. Let me begin at the beginning. Time was when Sir Zamran and the Lady Fevzi were lovers, all right and decorous in accord with the customs of the Order. Then for some reason Lady Fevzi cast off Zamran, as she had every right to do, and took Sir Shurgez in his stead. This made Sir Zamran wroth, and instead of taking his defeat philosophically like a true knight, what does he do but come up behind Lady Fevzi at the ball celebrating the conjunction of the planets Vishnu and Ganesha, and smite off her head just as she was presenting a homemade pie to the grand master!"

"Wow!" said Borel with an honest shudder.

"True, 'twas no knightly deed, especially in front of the grand master, not to mention the difficulty of cleansing the carpet. If he had to slay her he should at least have taken her outside. The grand master, most annoyed, would have rebuked Zamran severely for his discourtesy, but he's hardly past the preamble when Sir Shurgez comes in to ask after his sweetling, sees the scene, and leaps upon Zamran with his dagger before any can stay him. So then we have two spots on the rug to clean and the grand master in a fair fury. The upshot was that he ordered Shurgez on this quest to teach him to issue his challenges in due form and not go thrusting knives among the ribs of any who incur his displeasure. No doubt he half hoped that Shurgez would be slain ill the doing, for the King of Balhib is no effeminate."

Borel was sure now that nothing would ever induce him to settle permanently among such violent people. "When did Shurgez get time to—uh—be friends with Zerdai?"

"Why, he couldn't leave before the astrological indications were favorable, to wit for twenty-one days, and during that time he enjoyed my secretary's favor. Far places have ever attracted her, and I think she'd have gone with him if he'd have had her."

"What's the word about Shurgez now?"

"The simplest word of all, to wit: no word. Should he return, my spies will tell me of his approach before he arrives."

Borel became aware that the clicking sound that had puzzled him was the chatter of his own teeth. He resolved to ride herd on Henjare the next day to rush the model through to completion.

"One more question," he said. "Whatever became of Lady Fevzi's pie?" Kubanan could not tell him that, however.

THE MODEL was in fact well enough so that Borel asked the grand master for the perpetual motion meeting the following day. Although he expected an evening meeting, with all the knights full of dinner and feeling friendly, it turned out that the only time available on the grand master's schedule was in the morning.

"Of course, Brother Felix," said Sir Djuvain, "if you prefer to put it off a few days…"

"No, most mighty potentate," said Borel, thinking of the Shurgez menace. "The sooner the better for you, me, and the Order."

Thus it happened that the next morning, after breakfast, Felix Borel found himself on the platform of the main auditorium of the citadel, facing several thousand knights of the Order of Qarar. Beside him on a small table stood his gleaming new brass model of the perpetual motion wheel. A feature of the wheel not obvious to the audience was a little pulley on the shaft, around which was wound a fine but strong thread made of hairs from the tails of shomals, which led from the wheel off into the wings where Zerdai stood hidden from view. It had taken all Borel's blandishments to get her to play this role.

He launched into his speech: "…what is the purpose and function of our noble Order? Power! And what is the basis of power? First, our own strong right arms; second, the wealth of the Order, which in turn is derived from the wealth of the commons. So anything that enriches the commons increases our power, does it not? Let me give you an example. There's a railroad, I hear, from Madjbur to Djazmurian along the coast, worked by bishtars pulling little strings of cars. Now, mount one of my wheels on a car and connect it by a belt or chain to the wheels. Start the wheel revolving, and what happens? The car with its wheel will pull far more cars than a bishtar, and likewise it never grows old and dies as an animal does, never runs amok and smashes property, and when not in use stands quietly in its shed without needing to be fed. We could build a railroad from Mishe to Madjbur and another from Mishe to Djazmurian, and carry goods faster between the coastal cities than it is now carried by the direct route. There's a source of infinite wealth, of which the Order would of course secure its due share.

"Then there is the matter of weapons. I cannot go into details because many of these are confidential, but I have positive assurance that there are those who would trade the mighty weapons of the Interplanetary Council for the secret of this little wheel. You know what that would mean. Think it over.

"Now I will show you how it actually works. This model you see is not a true working wheel, but a mere toy, an imitation to give you an idea of the finished wheel, which would be much larger. This little wheel will not give enough power to be very useful. Why? Friction. The mysterious sciences of my native planet found centuries ago that friction is proportionately larger in small machines than in large ones. Therefore the fact that this little wheel won't give useful power is proof that a larger one would.

However, the little wheel still gives enough power to run itself without outside help.

"Are you watching closely, brothers? I want you to observe: I release the brake that—as you can see—prevents the wheel from turning. Hold your breaths, sirs—ah, it moves! It turns! The secret of the ages comes to life before you!"

HE HAD signaled Zerdai, who had begun to pull on the thread, reeling in one end of it while paying out the other. The wheel turned somewhat slowly, the little brass legs going click-click-click as they reached the trip at the top.

"Behold!" yelled Borel. "It works! The Order is all-rich and all-powerful!"

After letting the wheel spin for a minute or so, Borel resumed: "Brothers, what must we do to realize on this wonderful invention,? One, we need funds to build a number of large wheels to tryout various applications: to power ships and rail cars, to run gristmills, and to turn the shafts of machines in workshops. No machine is ever perfect when first completed; there are always details to be improved. Second, we need an organization to exploit the wheel—to make treaties with other states to lease wheels from us and to give us the exclusive right to exploit wheels within their borders; and to negotiate with the powers that be to exchange the secret of the wheel for—I need go no further!

"On Earth we have a type of organization called a corporation for such purposes..." And be launched into the account he had previously given to both Kubanan and Djuvain.

"Now then," he said, "what is it exactly that we need for this corporation? The officers of the Order and I have agreed that to start, the treasury shall advance the sum of 245,000 *karda,* for which the Order shall receive forty-nine percent of the stock of the company. The remaining fifty-one percent will naturally remain with the promoter and director of the company; that's the arrangement we've found to be the most successful on Earth. However, before such a significantly large sum can be invested in this great enterprise, we must, in accordance with the constitution, let you vote on the question. First I had better stop our little wheel here, lest the noise distract you."

The clicking stopped as Borel put his hand against the wheel. Zerdai broke the thread with a quick jerk, gathered it all in, and slipped away from her hiding place.

Borel continued: "I therefore turn the meeting back to our friend, guide, counselor, and leader, Grand Master Sir Djuvain."

The Grand Master put the vote and the appropriation passed by a large majority. As the knights cheered, Kubanan led a line of pages staggering under bags of coins to the stage, where the bags were ranged in a row on the boards.

Borel, when he could get silence again, said: "I thank you one and all. If any would care to examine my little wheel, they shall see for themselves that no trickery is involved."

The *Garma Qararuma* climbed up *en masse* to congratulate Borel. The adventurer, trying not to seem to gloat over the money, was telling himself that once he got away with this bit of swag he'd sell it for World Federation dollars, go on back to Earth, invest his fortune most conservatively, and never have to worry about money again for the rest of his life. Of course he'd promised himself the same thing on a number of previous occasions, but somehow the money always seemed to dissipate before he got around to investing it.

CHAPTER FIVE

SIR VOLHADJ was pushing through the crowd, saying:
"Sir Felix, may I speak to you aside?"

"Sure. What is it?"

"How feel you?"

"Fine. Never better."

"That's good, for Shurgez has returned to Mishe with his mission accomplished."

"What's that?" said Kubanan.

"Shurgez back, and my spies haven't told me?"

"Right, my lord."

"Oh-oh," said the treasurer. "If he challenges you, Sir Felix, you will, as a knight, have to give him instant satisfaction. What arms own you besides that sword?"

"Gluk," said Borel. "N-none. Doesn't the challenge party have a choice of weapons?" he asked with some vague idea of specifying boxing gloves.

"According to the rules of the Order," said Volhadj, "each fighter may use what weapons he pleases. Shurgez will indubitably employ the full panoply: lance, sword, and a mace or ax in reserve, and will enter the lists in full armor. As for you—well, since you and I are much of a size, feel free to borrow aught that you need."

Before Borel could say anything more, a murmur and a head turning apprised him of the approach of some interest. As the crowd parted, a squat, immensely muscular, and very Mongoloid-looking knight came forward. "Are you he whom they call Sir Felix the Red?" asked the newcomer.

"Y-yes," said Borel, icicles of fear running through his viscera.

"I am Sir Shurgez. It has been revealed to me that in my absence you've taken the Lady Zerdai as your companion. Therefore I name you a vile traitor, scurvy knave, villainous rascal, base mechanic, and foul foreigner, and shall be at the tournament-grounds immediately after lunch to prove my assertions upon your diseased and ugly body. Here, you thing of no account!" And Sir Shurgez, who had been peeling off his glove, threw it lightly in Borel's face.

"I'll fight you," shouted Borel in a sudden surge of temper. *"Beghan! Zeft!"* He added a few more Gozashtandou obscenities and threw the glove back at Shurgez, who caught it, laughed shortly, and turned his back.

"That's that," said Kubanan as Shurgez marched off. "Sure am I that so bold and experienced a knight as yourself will make mincemeat of yon braggart. Shall I have my pages convey the gold to your chamber while we lunch?"

Borel felt like saying: "I don't want any lunch," but judged it impolitic. His wits, after the first moment of terror-stricken paralysis, had begun to work again. First he felt sorry for himself. What had he done to deserve this? Why had he joined this crummy club, where instead of swindling each other like gentlemen the members settled differences by the cruel and barbarous methods of physical combat? All he'd done was to keep Zerdai happy while this blug was away...

Then he pulled himself together and tried to think his way out of the predicament. Should he simply refuse to fight? That meant skinning alive. Could he sprain an ankle? Maybe, but with all these people standing around… Why hadn't he told that well-meaning sap Volhadj that he was sick unto death?

And now how could he get away with the gold? It was probably too heavy for the buggy; he'd need a big two-aya carriage, which couldn't be obtained in a matter of minutes. How could he make his getaway at all before the fight? With his dear damned friends clustering round…

They were filling him with good advice: "I knew a man who'd begin a charge with lance level, then whirl it around his head as 'twere a club…" "When. Sir Vardao slew that wight from Gozashtand, he dropped his lance altogether and snatched his mace…" "If you can get him around the neck with one arm, go for his crotch with your dagger…"

What he really wanted was advice on how to sneak out of the acropolis and make tracks for Novorecife with a third of the Order's treasury. When he had gulped the last tasteless morsel, he said: "Good sirs, please excuse me. I have things to say to those near to me."

ZERDAI was crying on her bed. He picked her up and kissed her. She responded avidly; this was an Earthly custom on which the Krishnans had eagerly seized.

"Come," he said, "it's not that bad."

She clung to him frantically. "But I love only you! I couldn't live without you! And I've been counting so on going with you to far planets…"

Borel's vestigial conscience stirred, and in a rare burst of frankness he said: "Look, Zerdai, it'll be small loss no matter how the fight comes out. I'm not the shining hero you think I am; in fact some people consider me an unmitigated heel."

"No! No! You're kind and good..."

"...and even if I get through this alive I may have to run for it without you."

"I'll die! I could never companion with that brute Shurgez again..."

Borel thought of giving her some of the gold, since he couldn't hope to get it all away himself. But then with the Guardians' communistic principles she couldn't keep it, and the Order would seize all he left in any case. Finally he unpinned several of his more glittery decorations and handed them to her, saying:

"At least you'll have these to remember me by." That seemed to break her down completely.

He found Yerevats in his own room and said: "If the fight doesn't go my way, take as much of this gold as you can carry, and the buggy, and get out of town fast."

"Oh, wonderful master must win fight!"

"That's as the stars decide. Hope for the best but expect the worse."

"But master, how shall pull buggy?"

"Keep the aya too. Volhadj is lending me his oversized one for the scrap. Tell you what, when we go out to the field, bring one of those bags inside your clothes."

AN HOUR later Yerevats buckled the last strap of Borel's borrowed harness. The suit was a composite, chain mail over the joints and plate-armor elsewhere. Borel found that it hampered him less than be expected, considering how heavy it had seemed when he hefted before putting it on.

He stepped out of the tent at his end of the field, where Volhadj was holding the big aya, which turned and looked at him suspiciously from under its horns. At the far end Shurgez already sat on his mount. Borel, though outwardly calm, was reviling himself for not having thought of this and that: he should have hinted that his weapon would be a gun; he should have bought a bishtar and sat high up on its elephantine back, out of reach of Shurgez, while he potted his enemy with his crossbow...

Yerevats, bustling about the animal's saddle, secured the bag he had brought with him. Although he tried to do so secretly, the jingle of coins attracted the attention of Volhadj who asked : "A bag of gold on your saddle? Why do you that, friend?"

"Luck," said Borel, feeling for the stirrup. His first effort to swing his leg over his mount failed because of the extra weight he was carrying, and they had to give him a boost. Yerevats handed him up his spiked helmet, which he carefully wiggled down onto his head. At once the outside noises acquired a muffled quality as the sound was filtered through the steel and the padding. Borel buckled his chinstrap.

A horn blew. As he had seen the other knights do the day of the previous battle, Borel kicked the animal into motion and rode slowly down the field towards his opponent, who advanced to meet him. Thank the Lord he knew how to ride an Earthly horse! This was not much different save that the fact that the saddle was directly over the aya's intermediate pair of legs caused its rider to be jarred unpleasantly in the trot.

Borel could hardly recognize Shurgez behind the nasal of his helmet, and he supposed that his own features were equally hidden. Without a word they wheeled towards the side of the field where the grand master sat in his booth. They walked their animals over to the stand and listened side by side while Sir Djuvain droned the rules of the contest at them. Borel thought it an awful lot of words to say that, for all practical purposes, anything went.

Beside the grand master sat Kubanan, stony-faced except at the last, when he tipped Borel a wink. Borel also caught a glimpse of Zerdai in the stands; catching his eye, she waved frantically.

The grand master finished and made motions with his baton. The fighters wheeled away from each other and trotted back to their respective tents, where Volhadj handed Borel his lance and buckler, saying: "Hold your shaft level; watch his..." Borel, totally preoccupied, heard none of it.

"Get you ready," said Volhadj. The trumpet blew.

Borel, almost bursting with excitement, said: "Goodbye, and thanks."

THE HOOVES of Shurgez's mount were already drumming on the moss before Borel collected his wits enough to put his own beast into motion. For a long time, it seemed, he rode towards a little figure on aya-back that got no nearer. Then all at once the aya and its rider expanded to life-size and Borel's foe was upon him.

Since Shurgez had started sooner and ridden harder, they met short of the mid-point of the field. As his enemy bore down, Borel rose in his stirrups and threw his lance at Shurgez, then instantly hauled on the reins braided into the aya's mustache to guide it to the right.

Shurgez ducked as the lance hurtled toward him, so that the point of his own lance wavered and missed Borel by a meter. Borel heard the thrown spear hit sideways with a clank against Shurgez's armor. Then he was past and headed for Shurgez's tent at the far end. He leaned forward and spurred his aya mercilessly.

Just before he reached the end of the field he jerked a look back. Shurgez was still reining in to turn his mount. Borel switched his attention back to where he was going and aimed for a gap on one side of Shurgez's tent. The people around the tent stood staring until the last minute, then frantically dove out of the way as the aya thundered through. Yells rose behind.

Borel guided his beast over to the main road towards Novorecife, secured the reins to the projection on the front of the saddle, and began shedding impedimenta. Off went the pretty damascened helmet, to fall with a clank to the roadway. Away went sword and battle-ax. After some fumbling he got rid of the brassets on his forearms and their attached gauntlets, and then the cuirass with its little chain sleeves. The iron pants would have to await a better opportunity.

The aya kept on at a dead run until Mishe dwindled in the distance. When the beast began to puff alarmingly, Borel let it slow to a walk for a while. However, when he looked back he thought he saw little dots on the road that might be pursuers, and spurred his mount to a gallop once more. When the dots disappeared he slowed again. Gallop-trot-walk-trot-gallop—that was how you covered long distances on a horse, so it should work on this six-legged equivalent. Oh for a nice shiny Packard! After this he'd confine his effort to Earth, where at least you knew the score.

He looked scornfully down at the bag of gold clinking faintly at the side of his saddle. One bag was all he had dared to take for fear of slowing his mount. It was not a bad haul for small-time stuff, and would let him live and travel long enough to case his next set of suckers. Still, it was nothing compared to what he'd have made if the damned Shurgez hadn't popped up so inopportunely. If, now, he'd been able to get away with the proceeds both of the stock sale and of the lottery...

NEXT MORNING found Borel still on the aya's back, plodding over the causeway through the Koloft Swamps. Flying things buzzed and bit; bubbles of stinking gas rose through the black water and burst. Now and then some sluggish swamp-dwelling creature roiled the surface or grunted a mating call. A shower had soaked Borel during the night, and in this dank atmosphere his clothes seemed never to dry.

With yelping cries, the tailed men of Koloft broke from the bushes and ran towards him: Yerevats's wild brethren with stone-bladed knives and spears, hairy, naked, and fearful-looking. Borel spurred the aya into a shambling trot. The tailed men scrambled to the causeway just too late to seize him; a thrown spear went past his head with a swish.

Borel threw away his kindness-to-animals principle and dug spurs into the aya's flanks. They pounded after him. In fact by squirming around he could see that they were actually gaining on him. Another spear came whistling along. Borel flinched, and the spearhead struck the cantle of his saddle and broke, leaving a sliver of obsidian sticking into the saddle as the shaft clattered to the causeway. The next one, he thought gloomily, would be a hit.

Then inspiration seized him. If he could get his moneybag open and throw a handful of gold to the roadway, these savages might stop to scramble for it. His fingers tore at Yerevats's lashings.

And then the twenty-kilo weight of the gold snatched the whole bag from his grasp. Clank! Gold pieces spilled out of the open mouth of the sack and rolled in little circles on the causeway. The tailed men whooped and pounced on them, abandoning their chase. While Borel was glad not to have to dodge any more spears, he did think the price a little steep. However, to go back to dispute possession of the money now would be merely a messy form of suicide, so he rode wearily on.

He reeled into Novorecife about noon, and was no sooner inside the wall than a man in the uniform of Abreu's security force said: "Is the senhor Felix Borel?"

"Huh?" He had been thinking in Gozashtandou so long that in his exhausted state the Brazilo-Portuguese of the spaceways at first was entirely meaningless to him.

"I said, is the senhor Felix Borel ?"

"Yes. Sir Felix Borel to be exact. What—"

"I don't care what the senhor calls himself; he's under arrest."

"What for?"

"Violation of Regulation 368. *Vamos, por favor!*"

BOREL demanded a lawyer at the preliminary hearing, and since he could not pay for one, Judge Keshavachandra appointed Manuel Sandak. Abreu presented his case.

Borel asked: "Senhor Abreu, how the devil did you find out about this little project of mine so quickly?"

The judge said: "Address your remarks to the court, please. The Security Office has its methods, naturally. Have you anything pertinent to say?"

Borel whispered to Sandak, who rose and said: "It is the contention of the defense that the case presented by the Security Office is *prima facie* invalid, because the device in question, to wit: a wheel allegedly embodying the principle of perpetual motion, is inherently inoperative, being in violation of the well known law of conservation of energy. Regulation 368 specifically states that it's forbidden to communicate a device representing an improvement upon the science and techniques already existing upon this planet. But since this gadget wouldn't work by any stretch of the imagination it's no improvement on anything."

"You mean," sputtered Abreu, "that it was all a fake, a swindle?"

"Sure," said Borel, laughing heartily at the security officer's expression.

Abreu said: "My latest information says that you actually demonstrated the device the day before yesterday in the auditorium of the Order of Qarar at Mishe. What have you to say to that?"

"That was a fake too," said Borel, and told of the thread pulled by Zerdai in the wings.

"Just how is this gadget supposed to work?" asked the judge. Borel explained. Keshavachandra exclaimed:

"Good Lord, that form of perpetual motion device goes back to the European Middle Ages! I remember a case involving it when I was a patent lawyer in India." He turned to Abreu, saying: "Does that description check with your information?"

"Sim, Vossa Excelencia." He turned on Borel. "I knew you were a crook, but I never expected you to brag on the fact as part of a legal charge!"

"Bureaucrat!" sneered Borel.

"No personalities," snapped Judge Keshavachandra. "I'm afraid I can't bind him over, Senhor Cristovao."

"How about a charge of swindling?" said Abreu hopefully.

Sandak jumped up. "You can't, your honor. The act was committed in Mikardand, so this court has no jurisdiction."

"How about holding him until we see if the Republic wants him back?" said Abreu.

Sandak said: "That won't work either. We have no extradition treaty with Mikardand because their legal code doesn't meet the minimum requirements of the Interplanetary Juridical Commission. Moreover the courts hold that a suspect may not be forcibly returned to a jurisdiction where he'd be liable to be killed on sight."

The judge said: "I'm afraid he's right again, Senhor. However we still have some power over undesirables. Draw me a request for an expulsion order and I'll sign it quicker than you can say 'non vult'. There are ships leaving in a few days, and we can give him his choice of them. I dislike inflicting him on other jurisdictions, but I don't know what else we can do." He added with a broad smile: "He'll probably turn up here again like a bad anna, with a cop three jumps behind him. Talk of perpetual motion, he's it!"

BOREL slouched into the Nova Iorque Bar and ordered a double comet. He fished his remaining money out of his pants pocket: about four and a half karda. This might feed him until he took off. Or it might provide him with a first-class binge. He decided on the binge; if he got drunk enough he wouldn't care about food in the interim.

He caught a glimpse of himself in the mirror back of the bar, unshaven, with eyes as red as his hair and his gorgeous private uniform unpressed and weather-beaten. Most of the bravado had leaked out of him. If he'd avoided the Noverecife jail, he was still about to be shipped to who knew where, without even a stake to get started again. The fact that he was getting his transportation free gave him no pleasure, for he knew space travel for the ineffable bore it was.

Now that Zerdai was irrevocably lost to him, he kidded himself into thinking that he'd really intended to take her with him as he'd promised. He wallowed in self-pity. Maybe he should even go to work, repugnant though the idea appeared. (He always thought of reforming when he got into a jam like this.) But who'd employ him around Novorecife when he was in Abreu's black books? To go back to Mikardand would be silly. Why hadn't he done this, or that…

Borel became aware of a man drinking down the bar; a stout middle-aged person with a look of sleepy good nature.

Borel said: "New here, senhor?"

"Yes," said the man. "I just came in two days ago from Earth."

"Good old Earth," said Borel.

"Good old Earth is right."

"Let me buy you a drink," said Borel.

"I will if you'll let me buy you one."

"Maybe that can be arranged. How long are you here for?"

"I don't know yet."

"What do you mean, you don't know yet?"

"I'll tell you. When I arrived, I wanted a good look at the planet. But now I've finished my official business and seen everything in Novorecife, and I can't go wandering around the native states because I don't speak the languages. I hoped to pick up a guide, but everybody seems too busy at some job of his own."

Borel, instantly alert, asked: "What sort of tour did you have in mind?"

"Oh, through the Gozashtandou Empire, perhaps touching the Free City of Madjbur, and maybe swinging around to Balhib on my way back."

"That would be a swell tour," said Borel. "Of course it would take you through some pretty wild country, and you'd have to ride an aya. No carriages. Also there'd be some risk."

"That's all right. I've ridden a horse ever since I was a boy. As for the risk, I've had a couple of centuries already, and I might as well have some fun before I get really old."

"Have another," said Borel. "You know, we might be able to make a deal on that. I just finished a job. My name's Felix Borel, by the way."

"I'm Semion Trofimov," said the man. "Would you be seriously interested in acting as a guide? I thought from your rig that you were some official…"

Borel barely heard the rest. Semion Trofimov! A big-shot if ever there was one; a director of *Viagens Interplanetarias,* member of various public boards and commissions, officer of capitalistic and cooperative enterprises back on Earth… At least there'd be no question of the man's ability to pay well, and to override these local bureaucrats who wanted to ship Borel anywhere so long as it was a few light years away.

"Sure, Senhor Semion," he said. "I'll give you a tour such as no Earthman ever had. There's a famous waterfall in northern Ruz, for instance, that few Earthmen have seen. And then do you know how the Kingdom of Balhib is organized? A very interesting set-up. In fact I've often thought a couple of smart Earthmen with a little capital could start an enterprise there, all perfectly legal, and clean up. I'll explain it later. Meanwhile we'd better get our gear together. Got a sword? And a riding outfit? I know an honest Koloftu we can get for a servant, if I can find him, and I've got one aya already. As for that Balhib scheme, an absolutely sure thing..."

THE END

If you've enjoyed this book, you will not want to miss these terrific titles…

ARMCHAIR SCI-FI, FANTASY, & HORROR DOUBLE NOVELS, $12.95 each

D-1   **THE GALAXY RAIDERS** by William P. McGivern
        SPACE STATION #1 by Frank Belknap Long

D-2   **THE PROGRAMMED PEOPLE** by Jack Sharkey
        SLAVES OF THE CRYSTAL BRAIN by William Carter Sawtelle

D-3   **YOU'RE ALL ALONE** by Fritz Leiber
        THE LIQUID MAN by Bernard C. Gilford

D-4   **CITADEL OF THE STAR LORDS** by Edmund Hamilton
        VOYAGE TO ETERNITY by Milton Lesser

D-5   **IRON MEN OF VENUS** by Don Wilcox
        THE MAN WITH ABSOLUTE MOTION by Noel Loomis

D-6   **WHO SOWS THE WIND...** by Rog Phillips
        THE PUZZLE PLANET by Robert A. W. Lowndes

D-7   **PLANET OF DREAD** by Murray Leinster
        TWICE UPON A TIME by Charles L. Fontenay

D-8   **THE TERROR OUT OF SPACE** by Dwight V. Swain
        QUEST OF THE GOLDEN APE by Ivar Jorgensen and Adam Chase

D-9   **SECRET OF MARRACOTT DEEP** by Henry Slesar
        PAWN OF THE BLACK FLEET by Mark Clifton.

D-10 **BEYOND THE RINGS OF SATURN** by Robert Moore Williams
        A MAN OBSESSED by Alan E. Nourse

ARMCHAIR SCIENCE FICTION CLASSICS, $12.95 each

C-1   **THE GREEN MAN**
        by Harold M. Sherman

C-2   **A TRACE OF MEMORY**
        By Keith Laumer

C-3   **INTO PLUTONIAN DEPTHS**
        by Stanton A. Coblentz

ARMCHAIR MASTERS OF SCIENCE FICTION SERIES, $16.95 each

M-1   **MASTERS OF SCIENCE FICTION, Vol. One**
        Bryce Walton—"Dark of the Moon" and other tales

M-2   **MASTERS OF SCIENCE FICTION, Vol. Two**
        Jerome Bixby—"One Way Street" and other tales

If you've enjoyed this book, you will not want to miss these terrific titles…

ARMCHAIR SCI-FI & HORROR DOUBLE NOVELS, $12.95 each

D-11 **PERIL OF THE STARMEN** by Kris Neville
THE STRANGE INVASION by Murray Leinster

D-12 **THE STAR LORD** by Boyd Ellanby
CAPTIVES OF THE FLAME by Samuel R. Delany

D-13 **MEN OF THE MORNING STAR** by Edmund Hamilton
PLANET FOR PLUNDER by Hal Clement and Sam Merwin, Jr.

D-14 **ICE CITY OF THE GORGON** by Chester S. Geier and Richard Shaver
WHEN THE WORLD TOTTERED by Lester del Rey

D-15 **WORLDS WITHOUT END** by Clifford D. Simak
THE LAVENDER VINE OF DEATH by Don Wilcox

D-16 **SHADOW ON THE MOON** by Joe Gibson
ARMAGEDDON EARTH by Geoff St. Reynard

D-17 **THE GIRL WHO LOVED DEATH** by Paul W. Fairman
SLAVE PLANET by Laurence M. Janifer

D-18 **SECOND CHANCE** by J. F. Bone
MISSION TO A DISTANT STAR by Frank Belknap Long

D-19 **THE SYNDIC** by C. M. Kornbluth
FLIGHT TO FOREVER by Poul Anderson

D-20 **SOMEWHERE I'LL FIND YOU** by Milton Lesser
THE TIME ARMADA by Fox B. Holden

ARMCHAIR SCIENCE FICTION CLASSICS, $12.95 each

C-4 **CORPUS EARTHLING**
by Louis Charbonneau

C-5 **THE TIME DISSOLVER**
by Jerry Sohl

C-6 **WEST OF THE SUN**
by Edgar Pangborn

ARMCHAIR SCIENCE FICTION & HORROR GEMS SERIES, $12.95 each

G-1 **SCIENCE FICTION GEMS, Vol. One**
Isaac Asimov and others

G-2 **HORROR GEMS, Vol. One**
Carl Jacobi and others

If you've enjoyed this book, you will not want to miss these terrific titles...

If you've enjoyed this book, you will not want to miss these terrific titles…

ARMCHAIR SCI-FI & HORROR DOUBLE NOVELS, $12.95 each

ARMCHAIR SCIENCE FICTION & FANTASY CLASSICS, $12.95 each

If you've enjoyed this book, you will not want to miss these terrific titles…

ARMCHAIR SCI-FI & HORROR DOUBLE NOVELS, $12.95 each

D-71 **THE DEEP END** by Gregory Luce
TO WATCH BY NIGHT by Robert Moore Williams

D-72 **SWORDSMAN OF LOST TERRA** by Poul Anderson
PLANET OF GHOSTS by David V. Reed

D-73 **MOON OF BATTLE** by J. J. Allerton
THE MUTANT WEAPON by Murray Leinster

D-74 **OLD SPACEMEN NEVER DIE!** John Jakes
RETURN TO EARTH by Bryan Berry

D-75 **THE THING FROM UNDERNEATH** by Milton Lesser
OPERATION INTERSTELLAR by George O. Smith

D-76 **THE BURNING WORLD** by Algis Budrys
FOREVER IS TOO LONG by Chester S. Geier

D-77 **THE COSMIC JUNKMAN** by Rog Phillips
THE ULTIMATE WEAPON by John W. Campbell

D-78 **THE TIES OF EARTH** by James H. Schmitz
CUE FOR QUIET by Thomas L. Sherred

D-79 **SECRET OF THE MARTIANS** by Paul W. Fairman
THE VARIABLE MAN by Philip K. Dick

D-80 **THE GREEN GIRL** by Jack Williamson
THE ROBOT PERIL by Don Wilcox

ARMCHAIR SCIENCE FICTION CLASSICS, $12.95 each

C-25 **THE STAR KINGS**
by Edmond Hamilton

C-26 **NOT IN SOLITUDE**
by Kenneth Gantz

C-32 **PROMETHEUS II**
by S. J. Byrne

ARMCHAIR SCIENCE FICTION & HORROR GEMS SERIES, $12.95 each

G-7 **SCIENCE FICTION GEMS, Vol. Four**
Jack Sharkey and others

G-8 **HORROR GEMS, Vol. Four**
Seabury Quinn and others

If you've enjoyed this book, you will not want to miss these terrific titles...

THE CITY THAT RAN OFF THE MAP

The town of Superior, Ohio, certainly was living up to its name! In what was undoubtedly the most spectacular feat of the century, it simply picked itself up one night and rose two full miles above Earth! Radio messages stated simply that Superior had seceded from Earth. But Don Cort, stranded on that rising town, was beginning to suspect that nothing was simple about Superior except its citizens. Calmly they accepted their rise in the world as being due to one of their local townspeople, a crackpot professor. But after a couple of weeks of floating around, it began to be obvious that the professor had no idea how to get them down. So then it was up to Cort: either find a way to anchor Superior, or spend the rest of his days on the smallest—and the nuttiest— planet in the galaxy!

ABOUT RICHARD WILSON:

Richard Wilson was born in Huntington Station, New York, in 1920. He eventually became a well-known sci-fi novelist and short story writer. He was also a full-time newsman for Reuters international press service back in the '50s and early '60s. His novels included *30-Day Wonder* and *The Girls from Planet 5*. He also authored dozens of science-fiction short stories dating back to 1938.

Wilson was known for writing late at night in the attic workroom of his century-old ex-farmhouse, located just thirty-five miles from Times Square.

During his career, Wilson was nominated for several Hugo and Nebula Awards. He brought home the Nebula in 1968 for his novelette, "Mother to the World." Many of Wilson's works were laced with satire and wit. A reviewer for the *New York Times* once praised "his wacky humor," and the *New York Herald-Tribune*'s critic declared "there's not another male in the science-fiction field who can beat Wilson in the easy, intimate exposition of the private lives of the space-future." After a long career, Richard Wilson passed away in March of 1987.

AND THEN THE TOWN TOOK OFF

By
RICHARD WILSON

ARMCHAIR FICTION
PO Box 4369, Medford, Oregon 97501-0168

*For more information about Armchair Books and products, visit our
website at…*

www.armchairfiction.com

Or email us at…

armchairfiction@yahoo.com

CHAPTER ONE

The town of Superior, Ohio, disappeared on the night of October 31.

A truck driver named Pierce Knaubloch was the first to report it. He had been highballing west along Route 202, making up for the time he'd spent over a second cup of coffee in a diner, when he screeched to a stop. If he'd gone another twenty-five feet he'd have gone into the pit where Superior had been.

Knaubloch couldn't see the extent of the pit because it was too dark, but it looked big. Bigger than if a nitro truck had blown up, which was his first thought. He backed up two hundred feet, set out flares, then sped off to a telephone.

The state police converged on the former site of Superior from several directions. Communicating by radiophone across the vast pit, they confirmed that the town undoubtedly was missing. They put in a call to the National Guard.

The guard surrounded the area with troops—more than a thousand were needed—to keep people from falling into the pit. A pilot who flew over it reported that it looked as if a great ice-cream scoop had bitten into the Ohio countryside.

The Pennsylvania Railroad complained that one of its passenger trains was missing. The train's schedule called for it to pass through but not stop at Superior at 11:58. That seemed to fix the time of the disappearance at midnight. The truck driver had made his discovery shortly after midnight.

Someone pointed out that October 31 was Halloween and that midnight was the witching hour.

Somebody else said nonsense, they'd better check for radiation. A civil defense official brought up a Geiger counter, but no matter how he shook it and rapped on it, it refused to click.

A National Guard officer volunteered to take a jeep down into the pit, having found a spot that seemed navigable. He was gone a long time but when he came out the other side he reported that the pit was concave, relatively smooth, and did not smell of high explosives. He'd found no people, no houses—no sign of anything except the pit itself.

The Governor of Ohio asked Washington whether any unidentified planes had been over the state. Washington said no. The Pentagon and the Atomic Energy Commission denied that they had been conducting secret experiments.

Nor had there been any defense plants in Superior that might have blown up. The town's biggest factory made kitchen sinks and the next biggest made bubble gum.

A United Airlines pilot found Superior early on the morning of November 1. The pilot, Captain Eric Studley, who had never seen a flying saucer and hoped never to see one, was afraid now that he had. The object loomed out of a cloudbank at twelve thousand feet and Studley changed course to avoid it. He noted with only minimum satisfaction that his co-pilot also saw the thing and wondered why it wasn't moving at the terrific speed flying saucers were allegedly capable of.

Then he saw the church steeple on it.

A few minutes later he had relayed a message from Superior, formerly of Ohio, addressed to whom it might concern:

It said that Superior had seceded from Earth.

One other radio message came from Superior, now airborne, on that first day. A ham radio operator reported an unidentified voice as saying plaintively:

"*Cold* up here!"

Don Cort had been dozing in what passed for the club car on the Buckeye Cannonball when the train braked to a stop. He looked out the window, hoping this was Columbus, where he planned to catch a plane east. But it wasn't Columbus. All he could see were some lanterns jogging as trainmen hurried along the tracks.

The conductor looked into the car. The redhead across the aisle in whom Don had taken a passing interest earlier in the evening asked, "Why did we stop?"

"Somebody flagged us down," the conductor said. "We don't make a station stop at Superior on this run."

The girl's hair was a subtle red, but false. When Don had entered the club car he'd seen her hatless head from above and noticed that the hair along the part was dark. Her eyes had been on a book and Don had the opportunity for a brief study of her face. The cheeks were full and untouched by make-up. There were lines at the corners of her mouth which indicated a tendency to arrange her expression into one of disapproval. The lips were full, like the cheeks, but it was obvious that the scarlet lipstick had contrived a mouth a trifle bigger than the one nature had given her.

Her glance upward at that moment interrupted his examination, which had been about to go on to her figure. Later, though, he was able to observe that it was more than adequate.

If the girl had given Don Cort more than that one glance, or if it had been a trained, all-encompassing glance, she would have seen a man in his mid-twenties—about her age—lean, tall and straight-shouldered, with once-blond hair now verging on dark brown, a face neither handsome nor ugly, and a habit of drawing the inside of his left cheek between his teeth and nibbling at it thoughtfully.

But it was likely that all she noticed then was the brief case he carried, attached by a chain to a handcuff on his left wrist.

"Will we be here long?" Don asked the conductor. He didn't want to miss his plane at Columbus. The sooner he got to Washington, the sooner he'd get rid of the brief case. The handcuff it was attached to was one reason why his interest in the redhead had been only passing.

"Can't say," the conductor told him. He let the door close again and went down to the tracks.

Don hesitated, shrugged at the redhead, said, "Excuse me," and followed the conductor. About a dozen people were milling around the train as it sat in the dark, hissing steam. Don made his way up to the locomotive and found a bigger knot of people gathered in front of the cowcatcher.

Some sort of barricade had been put up across the tracks and it was covered with every imaginable kind of warning device. There were red lanterns, both battery and electric; flashlights; road flares; and even an old red shirt.

Don saw two men who must have been the engineer and the fireman talking to an old bearded gentleman wearing a civil defense helmet, a topcoat and riding boots.

"You'd go over the edge, I tell you," the old gentleman was saying.

"If you don't get this junk off the line," the engineer said, "I'll plow right through it. Off the edge! you crazy or something?"

"Look for yourself," the old man in the white helmet said. "Go ahead. Look."

The engineer was exasperated. He turned to the fireman. "You look. Humor the old man. Then let's go."

The bearded man—he called himself Professor Garet—went off with the fireman. Don followed them. They had tramped a quarter of a mile along the gravel when the fireman stopped. "Okay," he said "where's the edge? I don't see nothing." The tracks seemed to stretch forever into the darkness.

"It's another half mile or so," the professor said.

"Well, let's hurry up. We haven't got all night."

The old man chuckled. "I'm afraid you have."

They came to it at last, stopping well back from it. Professor Garet swelled with pride, it seemed, as he made a theatrical gesture.

"Behold," he said. "Something even Columbus couldn't find. The edge of the world."

True, everything seemed to stop, and they could see stars shining low on the horizon where stars could not properly be expected to be seen.

Don Cort and the fireman walked cautiously toward the edge while the professor ambled ahead with the familiarity of one who had been there before. But there was a wind and they did not venture too close. Nevertheless, Don could see that it apparently was a neat, sharp edge, not one of your old ragged, random edges such as might have been caused by an explosion. This one had the feeling of design behind it.

Standing on tiptoe and repressing a touch of giddiness, Don looked over the edge. He didn't have to stand on tiptoe any more than he had to sit on the edge of his seat during the exciting part of a movie, but the situation seemed to call for it. Over the edge could be seen a big section of Ohio. At least he supposed it was Ohio.

Don looked at the fireman, who had an unbelieving expression on his face, then at the bearded old man, who was smiling and nodding.

"You see what I mean," he said. "You would have gone right over. I believe you would have had a two-mile fall."

"Of course you could have stayed aboard the train," the man driving the old Pontiac said, "but I really think you'll be more comfortable at Cavalier."

Don Cort, sitting in the back seat of the car with the redhead from the club car, asked, "Cavalier?"

"The college. The institute, really; it's not accredited. What did you say your name was, miss?"

"Jen Jervis," she said. "Geneva Jervis, formally."

"Miss Jervis. I'm Civek. You know Mr. Cort, I suppose."

The girl smiled sideways. "We have a nodding acquaintance." Don nodded and grinned.

"There's plenty of room in the dormitories," Civek said. "People don't exactly pound on the gates and scream to be admitted to Cavalier."

"Are you connected with the college?" Don asked.

"Me? No. I'm the mayor of Superior. The old town's really come up in the world, hasn't it?"

"Overnight," Geneva Jervis said. "If what Mr. Cort and the fireman say is true. I haven't seen the edge myself."

"You'll have a better chance to look at it in the morning," the mayor said, "if we don't settle back in the meantime."

"Was there any sort of explosion?" Don asked.

"No. There wasn't any sensation at all, as far as I noticed. I was watching the late show—or trying to. My house is down in a hollow and reception isn't very good, especially with old English movies. Well, all of a sudden the picture sharpened up and I could see just as plain. Then the phone rang and it was Professor Garet."

"The old fellow with the whiskers and the riding boots?" Jen Jervis asked.

"Yes. Osbert Garet, Professor of Magnology at the Cavalier Institute of Applied Sciences."

"Professor of what?"

"Magnology. As I say, the school isn't accredited. Well, Professor Garet telephoned and said, 'Hector'—that's my name, Hector Civek—'everything's up in the air.' He was having his little joke, of course. I said, 'What?' and then he told me."

"Told you what?" Jen Jervis asked. "I mean, does he have any theory about it?"

"He has a theory about everything. I think what he was trying to convey was that this—this levitation confirmed his magnology principle."

"What's that?" Don asked.

"I haven't the faintest idea. I'm a politician, not a scientist. Professor Garet went on about it for a while, on the telephone, about magnetism and gravity, but I think he was only calling as a courtesy, so the mayor wouldn't look foolish the next morning, not knowing his town had flown the coop."

"What's the population of Superior?"

"Three thousand, including the students at the institute. Three thousand and forty, counting you people from the train. I guess you'll be with us for a while."

"What do you mean by that?" Jen Jervis asked.

"Well, I don't see how you can get down. Do you?"

"Does Superior have an airport?" Don asked. "I've got to get back to—to Earth." It sounded odd to put it that way.

"Nope," Civek said. "No airport. No place for a plane to land, either."

"Maybe not a plane," Don said, "but a helicopter could land just about anywhere."

"No helicopters here, either."

"Maybe not. But I'll bet they're swarming all over you by morning."

"Hm," said Hector Civek. Don couldn't quite catch his expression in the rearview mirror. "I suppose they could, at that. Well, here's Cavalier. You go right in that door, where the others are going. There's Professor Garet. I've got to see him—excuse me."

The mayor was off across the campus. Don looked at Geneva Jervis, who was frowning. "Are you thinking," he asked, "that Mayor Civek was perhaps just a little less than completely honest with us?"

"I'm thinking," she said, "that I should have stayed with Aunt Hattie another night, then taken a plane to Washington."

"Washington?" Don said. "That's where I'm going. I mean where I *was* going before Superior became airborne. What do you do in Washington, Miss Jervis?"

"I work for the Government. Doesn't everybody?"

"Not everybody. Me, for instance."

"No?" she said. "Judging by that satchel you're handcuffed to, I'd have thought you were a courier for the Pentagon. Or maybe State."

He laughed quickly and loudly because she was getting uncomfortably close. "Oh, no. Nothing so glamorous. I'm a messenger for the Riggs National Bank, that's all. Where do you work?"

"I'm with Senator Bobby Thebold, S.O.B."

Don laughed again. "He sure is."

"*Mister* Cort!" she said, annoyed. "You know as well as I do that S.O.B. stands for Senate Office Building. I'm his secretary."

"I'm sorry. We'd better get out and find a place to sleep. It's getting late."

"*Places* to sleep," she corrected. She looked angry.

"Of course," Don said, puzzled by her emphasis. "Come on. Where they put you, you'll probably be surrounded by co-eds, even if I could get out of this cuff."

He took her bag in his free hand and they were met by a gray-haired woman who introduced herself as Mrs. Garet. "We'll try to make you comfortable," she said. "What a night, eh? The professor is simply beside himself. We haven't had so much excitement since the cosmolineator blew up."

They had a glimpse of the professor, still in his CD helmet, going around a corner, gesticulating wildly to someone wearing a white laboratory smock.

CHAPTER TWO

Don Cort had slept, but not well. He had tried to fold the brief case to pull it through his sleeve so he could take his coat off, but whatever was inside the brief case was too big. Cavalier had given him a room to himself at one end of a dormitory and he'd taken his pants off but had had to sleep with his coat and shirt on. He got up, feeling gritty, and did what little dressing was necessary.

It was eight o'clock, according to the watch on the unhandcuffed wrist, and things were going on. He had a view of the campus from his window. A bright sun shone on young people moving generally toward a squat building, and other people going in random directions. The first were students going to breakfast, he supposed, and the others were faculty members. The air was very clear and the long morning shadows distinct. Only then did he remember completely that he and the whole town of Superior were up in the air.

He went through the dormitory. A few students were still sleeping. The others had gone from their unmade beds. He shivered as he stepped outdoors. It was crisp, if not freezing, and his breath came out visibly. First he'd eat, he decided, so he'd be strong enough to go take a good look over the edge, in broad daylight, to the Earth below.

The mess hall, or whatever they called it, was cafeteria style and he got in line with a tray for juice, eggs and coffee. He saw no one he knew, but as he was looking for a table a willowy blonde girl smiled and gestured to the empty place opposite her.

"You're Mr. Cort," she said. "Won't you join me?"

"Thanks," he said, unloading his tray. "How did you know?"

"The mystery man with the handcuff. You'd be hard to miss. I'm Alis—that's A-l-i-s, not A-l-i-c-e—Garet. Are you with the FBI? Or did you escape from jail?"

"How do you do. No, just a bank messenger. What an unusual name. Professor Garet's daughter?"

"The same," she said. "Also the only. A pity, because if there'd been two of us I'd have had a fifty-fifty chance of going to OSU. As it is, I'm duty-bound to represent the second generation at the nut factory."

"Nut factory? You mean Cavalier?" Don struggled to manipulate knife and fork without knocking things off the table with his clinging brief case.

"Here, let me cut your eggs for you," Alis said. "You'd better order them scrambled tomorrow. Yes, Cavalier. Home of the crackpot theory and the latter-day alchemist."

"I'm sure it's not that bad. Thanks. As for tomorrow, I hope to be out of here by then."

"How do you get down from an elephant? Old riddle. You don't; you get down from ducks. How do you plan to get down from Superior?"

"I'll find a way. I'm more interested at the moment in how I got up here."

"You were levitated, like everybody else."

"You make it sound deliberate, Miss Garet, as if somebody hoisted a whole patch of real estate for some fell purpose."

"Scarcely *fell*, Mr. Cort. As for it being deliberate, that seems to be a matter of opinion. Apparently you haven't seen the papers."

"I didn't know there were any."

"Actually there's only one, the *Superior Sentry*, a weekly. This is an extra. Ed Clark must have been up all night getting it out." She opened her purse and unfolded a four-page tabloid.

Don blinked at the headline:

Town Gets High

"Ed Clark's something of an eccentric, like everybody else in Superior," Alis said.

Don read the story, which seemed to him a capricious treatment of an apparently grave situation.

Residents having business beyond the outskirts of town today are advised not to. It's a long way down. Where Superior was surrounded by Ohio, as usual, today Superior ends literally at the town line.

A Citizens' Emergency Fence-Building Committee is being formed, but in the meantime all are warned to stay well away from the edge. The law of gravity seems to have been repealed for the town but it is doubtful if the same exemption would apply to a dubious individual bent on investigating...

Don skimmed the rest. "I don't see anything about it being deliberate."

Alis had been creaming and sugaring Don's coffee. She pushed it across to him and said, "It's not on page one. Ed Clark and Mayor Civek don't get along, so you'll find the mayor's statement in a box on page three, bottom."

Don creased the paper the other way, took a sip of coffee, nodded his thanks, and read:

Mayor Claims Secession From Earth

Mayor Hector Civek, in a proclamation issued locally by hand and dropped to the rest of the world in a plastic shatter-proof bottle, said today that Superior has seceded from Earth. His reasons were as vague as his explanation.

The "reasons" include these: (1) Superior has been discriminated against by county, state and federal agencies; (2) Cavalier Institute has been held up to global derision by orthodox (presumably meaning accredited) colleges and universities; and (3) chicle exporters have conspired against the Superior Bubble Gum Company by unreasonably raising prices.

The "explanation" consists of a 63-page treatise on applied magnology by Professor Osbert Garet of Cavalier which the editor (a) does not understand; (b) lacks space to publish; and which (it being atrociously handwritten) he (c) has not the temerity to ask his linotype operator to set.

Don said, "I'm beginning to like this Ed Clark."

"He's a doll," Alis said. "He's about the only one in town who stands up to Father."

"Does your father claim that *he* levitated Superior off the face of the Earth?"

"Not to me he doesn't. I'm one of those banes of his existence, a skeptic. He gave up trying to magnolize me when I was sixteen. I had a science teacher in high school—not in Superior, incidentally—who gave me all kinds of embarrassing questions to ask Father. I asked them, being a natural-born needler, and Father has disowned me intellectually ever since."

"How old are you, Miss Garet, if I may ask?"

She sat up straight and tucked her sweater tightly into her skirt, emphasizing her good figure. To a male friend Don would have described the figure as outstanding. She had mocking eyes, a pert nose and a mouth of such moist red softness that it seemed perpetually waiting to be kissed. All in all she could have been the queen of a campus much more densely populated with co-eds than Cavalier was.

"You may call me Alis," she said. "And I'm nineteen."

Don grinned. "Going on?"

"Three months past. How old are *you*, Mr. Cort?"

"Don's the name I've had for twenty-six years. Please use it."

"Gladly. And now, Don, unless you want another cup of coffee, I'll go with you to the end of the world."

"On such short notice?" Don was intrigued. Last night the redhead from the club car had repelled an advance that hadn't been made, and this morning a blonde was apparently making an advance that hadn't been solicited. He wondered where Geneva Jervis was, but only vaguely.

"I'll admit to the *double entendre*," Alis said. "What I meant—for now—was that we can stroll out to where Superior used to be attached to the rest of Ohio and see how the Earth is getting along without us."

"Delighted. But don't you have any classes?"

"Sure I do. Non-Einsteinian Relativity 1, at nine o'clock. But I'm a demon class-cutter, which is why I'm still a Senior at my advanced age. On to the brink!"

They walked south from the campus and came to the railroad track. The train was standing there with nowhere to go. It had been abandoned except for the conductor, who had dutifully spent the night aboard.

"What's happening?" he asked when he saw them. "Any word from down there?"

"Not that I know of," Don said. He introduced him to Alis Garet. "What are you going to do?"

"What *can* I do?" the conductor asked.

"You can go over to Cavalier and have breakfast," Alis said. "Nobody's going to steal your old train."

The conductor reckoned as how he might just do that, and did.

"You know," Don said, "I was half-asleep last night but before the train stopped I thought it was running alongside a creek for a while."

"South Creek," Alis said. "That's right. It's just over there."

"Is it still? I mean hasn't it all poured off the edge by now? Was that Superior's water supply?"

Alis shrugged. "All I know is you turn on the faucet and there's water. Let's go look at the creek."

They found it coursing along between the banks.

"Looks just about the same," she said.

"That's funny. Come on; let's follow it to the edge."

The brink, as Alis called it, looked even more awesome by daylight. Everything stopped short. There were the remnants of a cornfield, with the withered stalks cut down, then there was nothing. There was South Creek surging along, then nothing. In the distance a clump of trees, with a few autumn leaves still clinging to their branches, simply ended.

"Where is the water going?" Don asked. "I can't make it out."

"Down, I'd say. Rain for the Earth-people."

"I should think it'd be all dried up by now. I'm going to have a look."

"Don't! You'll fall off!"

"I'll be careful." He walked cautiously toward the edge. Alis followed him, a few feet behind. He stopped a yard from the brink and waited for a spell of dizziness to pass. The Earth was spread out like a topographer's map, far below. Don took another wary step, then sat down.

"Chicken," said Alis. She laughed uncertainly, then she sat down, too.

"I still can't see where the water goes," Don said. He stretched out on his stomach and began to inch forward. "You stay there."

Finally he had inched to a point where, by stretching out a hand, he could almost reach the edge. He gave another wriggle and the fingers of his right hand closed over the brink. For a moment he lay there, panting, head pressed to the ground.

"How do you feel?" Alis asked.

"Scared. When I get my courage back I'll pick up my head and look."

Alis put a hand out tentatively, then purposefully took hold of his ankle and held it tight. "Just in case a high wind comes along," she said.

"Thanks. It helps. Okay, here we go." He lifted his head. "Damn."

"What?"

"It still isn't clear. Do you have a pocket mirror?"

"I have a compact." She took it out of her bag with her free hand and tossed it to him. It rolled and Don had to grab to keep it from going over the edge. Alis gave a little shriek. Don was momentarily unnerved and had to put his head back on the ground. "Sorry," she said.

Don opened the compact and carefully transferred it to his right hand. He held it out beyond the edge and peered into it, focusing it on the end of the creek. "Now I've got it. The water *isn't* going off the edge!"

"It isn't? Then where is it going?"

"Down, of course, but it's as if it's going into a well, or a vertical tunnel, just short of the edge."

"Why? How?"

"I can't see too well, but that's my impression. Hold on now. I'm coming back." He inched away from the edge, then got up and brushed himself off. He returned her compact. "I guess you know where we go next."

"The other end of the creek?"

"Exactly."

South Creek did not bisect Superior, as Don thought it might, but flowed in an arc through a southern segment of it. They had about two miles to go, past South Creek Bridge—

which used to lead to Ladenburg, Alis said—past Raleigh Country Club (a long drive would really put the ball out of play, Don thought) and on to the edge again.

But as they approached what they were forced to consider the source of the creek, they found a wire fence at the spot. "This is new," Alis said.

The fence, which had a sign on it, warning—electrified, was semicircular, with each end at the edge and tarpaulins strung behind it so they could see the mouth of the creek. The water flowed from under the tarp and fence.

"Look how it comes in spurts," Alis said.

"As if it's being pumped."

Smaller print on the sign said: *Protecting mouth of South Creek, one of two sources of water for Superior. Electrical charge in fence is sufficient to kill.* It was signed: *Vincent Grande, Chief of Police, Hector Civek, Mayor.*

"What's the other source, besides the faucet in your bathroom?" Don asked.

"North Lake, maybe," Alis said. "People fish there but nobody's allowed to swim."

"Is the lake entirely within the town limits?"

"I don't know."

"If it were on the edge, and if I took a rowboat out on it, I wonder what would happen?"

"I know one thing—I wouldn't be there holding your ankle while you found out."

She took his arm as they gazed past the electrified fence at the Earth below and to the west.

"It's impressive, isn't it?" she said. "I wonder if that's Indiana way over there?"

He patted her hand absent-mindedly. "I wonder if it's west at all. I mean, how do we know Superior is maintaining the same position up here as it used to down there?"

"We could tell by the sun, silly."

"Of course," he said, grinning at his stupidity. "And I guess we're not high enough to see very far. If we were we'd be able to see the Great Lakes—or Lake Erie, anyway."

They were musing about the geography when a plane came out of a cloudbank and, a second later, veered sharply. They could make out UAL on the underside of a wing. As it turned they imagined they could see faces peering out of the windows. They waved and thought they saw one or two people wave back. Then the plane climbed toward the east and was gone.

"Well," Don said as they turned to go back to Cavalier, "now we know that they know. Maybe we'll begin to get some answers. Or, if not answers, then transportation."

"Transportation?" Alis squeezed the arm she was holding. "Why? Don't you like it here?"

"If you mean don't I like you, the answer is yes, of course I do. But if I don't get out of this handcuff soon so I can take a bath and get into clean clothes, you're not going to like me."

"You're still quite acceptable, if a bit whiskery." She stopped, still holding his arm, and he turned so they were face to face. "So kiss me," she said, "before you deteriorate."

They were in the midst of an extremely pleasant kiss when the brief case at the end of Don's handcuff began to talk to him.

CHAPTER THREE

Much of the rest of the world was inclined to regard the elevation of Superior, Ohio, as a Fortean phenomenon in the same category as flying saucers and sea monsters.

The press had a field day. Most of the headlines were whimsical:

Town Takes Off

Superior Lives Up To Name

A Rising Community

The city council of Superior, Wisconsin, passed a resolution urging its Ohio namesake to come back down. The Superiors in Nebraska, Wyoming, Arizona and West Virginia, glad to have the publicity, added their voices to the plea.

The Pennsylvania Railroad filed a suit demanding that the state of Ohio return forthwith one train and five miles of right-of-way.

The price of bubble gum went up from one cent to three for a nickel.

In Parliament a Labour member rose to ask the Home Secretary for assurances that all British cities were firmly fastened down.

An Ohio waterworks put in a bid for the sixteen square miles of hole that Superior had left behind, explaining that it would make a fine reservoir.

A company that leased out big advertising signs in Times Square offered Superior a quarter of a million dollars for exclusive rights to advertising space on its bottom, or

Earthward, side. It sent the offer by air mail, leaving delivery up to the post office.

In Washington, Senator Bobby Thebold ascertained that his red-haired secretary, Jen Jervis, had been aboard the train levitated with Superior and registered a series of complaints by telephone, starting with the Interstate Commerce Commission and the railroad brotherhoods. He asked the FBI to investigate the possibility of kidnaping and muttered about the likelihood of it all being a Communist plot.

A little-known congressman from Ohio started a rumor that raising of Superior was an experiment connected with the United States earth satellite program. The National Aeronautics and Space Administration issued a quick denial.

Two men talked earnestly in an efficient-looking room at the end of one of the more intricate mazes in the Pentagon Building. Neither wore a uniform but the younger man called the other sir, or chief, or general.

"We've established definitely that Sergeant Cort was on that train, have we?" the general asked.

"Yes, sir. No doubt about it."

"And he has the item with him?"

"He must have. The only keys are here and at the other end. He couldn't open the handcuff or the brief case."

"The only *known* keys, that is."

"Oh? How's that, General?"

"The sergeant can open the brief case and use the item if we tell him how."

"You think it's time to use it? I thought we were saving it."

"That was before Superior defected. Now we can use it to more advantage than any theoretical use it might be put to in the foreseeable future."

"We could evacuate Cort. Take him off in a helicopter or drop him a parachute and let him jump."

"No. Having him there is a piece of luck. No one knows who he is. We'll assign him there for the duration and have him report regularly. Let's go to the message center."

Senator Bobby Thebold was an imposing six feet two, a muscular 195, a youthful-looking 43. He wore his steel-gray hair cut short and his skin was tan the year round. He was a bachelor. He had been a fighter pilot in World War II and his conversation was peppered with Air Force slang, much of it out of date. Thebold was good newspaper copy and one segment of the press, admiring his fighting ways, had dubbed him Bobby the Bold. The Senator did not mind a bit.

At the moment Senator Thebold was pacing the carpet in the ample working space he'd fought to acquire in the Senate Office Building. He was momentarily at a loss. His inquiries about Jen Jervis had elicited no satisfaction from the ICC, the FBI, or the CIA. He was in an alphabetical train of thought and went on to consider the CAA, the CAB and the CAP. He snapped his fingers at CAP. He had it.

The Civil Air Patrol itself he considered a la-de-da outfit of gentleman flyers, skittering around in light planes, admittedly doing some good, but by and large nothing to excite a former P-38 pilot who'd won a chestful of ribbons for action in the Southwest Pacific.

Ah, but the PP. There was an organization! Bobby Thebold had been one of the founders of the Private Pilots, a hard-flying outfit that zoomed into the wild blue yonder on week ends and holidays, engines aroar, propellers aglint, white silk scarves aflap. PP's members were wealthy industrialists, stunt flyers, sportsmen—the elite of the air.

PP was a paramilitary organization with the rank of its officers patterned after the Royal Air Force. Thus Bobby Thebold, by virtue of his war record, his charter membership and his national eminence, was Wing Commander Thebold, DFC.

Wing Commander Thebold swung into action. He barked into the intercom: "Miss Riley! Get the airport. Have them rev up *Charger*. Tell them I'll be there for oh-nine-fifty-eight take-off. Ten-hundred will do. And get my car."

Charger was Bobby the Bold's war surplus P-38 Lightning, a sleek, twin-boomed two engine fighter plane restored to its gleaming, paintless aluminum. Actually it was an unarmed photo-reconnaissance version of the famous war horse of the Pacific, a fact the wing commander preferred to ignore. In compensation, he belted on a .45 whenever he climbed into the cockpit.

Thebold got onto Operations in PP's midwestern headquarters in Chicago. He barked, long distance:

"Jack Perley? Group Captain Perley, that is? Bobby, that's right. Wing Commander Thebold now. We've got a mission, Jack. Scramble Blue Squadron. What? Of course you can; this is an emergency. We'll rendezvous north of Columbus—I'll give you the exact grid in half an hour, when I'm airborne. Can do? Good-o! ETA? Eleven-twenty EST. Well, maybe that is optimistic, but I hate to see the day slipping by. Make it eleven-forty-five. What? Objective? Objective Superior! Got it? Okay—roger!"

Wing Commander Bobby Thebold took his Lindbergh-style helmet and goggles from a desk drawer, caressing the limp leather fondly, and put them in a dispatch case. He gave a soft salute to the door behind which Jen Jervis customarily worked, more as his second-in-command than his secretary, and said half aloud:

"Okay, Jen, we're coming to get you."

He didn't know quite how, but Bobby the Bold and Charger would soon be on their way.

Don Cort regretfully detached himself from Alis Garet.

"What was that?" he said.

"That was me—Alis the love-starved. You could be a bit more gallant. Even 'How was that?,' though corny, would have been preferable.

"No—I mean I thought I heard a voice. Didn't you hear anything?"

"To be perfectly frank—and I say it with some pique—I was totally absorbed. Obviously you weren't."

"It was very nice." The countryside, from the edge to the golf course, was deserted.

"Well, thanks. Thanks a bunch. Such enthusiasm is more than I can bear. I have to go now. There's an eleven o'clock class in magnetic flux that I'm simply dying to audit."

She gave her shoulder-length blonde hair a toss and started back. Don hesitated, looked suspiciously at the brief case dangling from his wrist, shook his head, then followed her. The voice, wherever it came from, had not spoken again.

"Don't be angry, Alis." He fell into step on her left and took her arm with his free hand. "It's just that everything is so crazy and nobody seems to be taking it seriously. A town doesn't just get up and take off, and yet nobody up here seems terribly concerned."

Alis squeezed the hand that held her arm, mollified. "You've got lipstick on your whiskers."

"Good. I'll never shave again."

"Ah," she laughed, "gallantry at last. I'll tell you what let's do. We'll go see Ed Clark, the editor of the Sentry. Maybe he'll give you some intelligent conversation."

The newspaper office was in a ramshackle one-story building on Lyric Avenue, a block off Broadway, Superior's main street. It was in an ordinary store front whose windows displayed various ancient stand-up cardboard posters calling attention to a church supper, a state fair, an auto race, and a movie starring H. B. Warner. A dust-covered banner urged the election as president of Alfred E. Smith.

There was no one in the front of the shop. Alis led Don to the rear where a tall skinny man with straggly gray hair was setting type.

"Good morning, Mr. Clark," she said. "What's that you're setting—an anti-Hoover handbill?"

"Hello, Al. How are you this fine altitudinous day?"

"Super. Or should it be supra? I want you to meet Don Cort. Don, Mr. Clark."

The men shook hands and Clark looked curiously at Don's handcuff.

"It's my theory he's an embezzler," Alis said, "and he's made this his getaway town."

"As a matter of fact," Don said, "the Riggs National Bank will be worried if I don't get in touch with them soon. I guess you'd know, Mr. Clark—is there any communication at all out of town?" By prearrangement, a message from Don to Riggs would be forwarded to Military Intelligence.

"I don't know of any, except for the Civek method—a bottle tossed over the edge. The telegraph and telephone lines are cut, of course. There is a radio station in town, WCAV, operated from the campus, but it's been silent ever since the great severance. At least nothing local has come over my old Atwater Kent."

"Isn't anybody *doing* anything?" Don asked.

"Sure," Clark said. "I'm getting out my paper—there was even an extra this morning—and doing job printing. The job is for a jeweler in Ladenburg. I don't know how I'll deliver it, but no one's told me to stop so I'm doing it. I guess everybody's carrying on pretty much as before."

"That's what I mean. Business as usual. But how about the people who do business out of town? What's Western Union doing, for instance? And the trucking companies?

And the factories? You have two factories, I understand, and pretty soon there's going to be a mighty big surplus of kitchen sinks and chewing gum."

"You two go on settling our fate," Alis said. "I'd better get back to school. Look me up later, Don." She waved and went out.

"Fine girl, that Alis," Clark said. "Got her old man's gumption without his nutty streak. To answer your question, the Western Union man here is catching up on his bookkeeping and accepting outgoing messages contingent on restoration of service. The sink factory made a shipment two days ago and won't have another ready till next week, so they're carrying on. They have enough raw material for a month. I was planning to visit the bubble gum people this afternoon to see how they're doing. Maybe you'd like to come."

"Yes, I would. I still chew it once in a while, on the sly."

Clark grinned. "I won't tell. Would you like to tidy up, Don? There's a washroom out back, with a razor and some mysterious running water. Now *there's* a phenomenon I'd like to get to the bottom of."

"Thanks. I'll shave with it now and worry about its source later. Do you think Professor Garet and his magnology cult has anything to do with it?"

"He'd like to think so, I'm sure." Clark shrugged. "We've been airborne less than twelve hours. I guess the answers will come in time. You go clean up and I'll get back to my job."

Don felt better when he had shaved. It had been awkward because he hadn't been able to take off his coat or shirt, but he'd managed. He was drying his face when the voice came again. This time there was no doubt it came from the brief case chained to his handcuff.

"Are you alone now?" it asked.

Startled, Don said, "Yes."

"Good. Speak closer to the brief case so we won't be overheard. This is Captain Simmons, Sergeant."

"Yes, sir."

"Take out your ID card. Separate the two pieces of plastic. There's a flat plastic key next to the card. Open the brief case lock with it."

The voice was silent until Don, with the help of a razor blade, had done as he was directed. "All right, sir; that's done."

"Open the brief case, take out the package, open the package and put the wrappings back in the brief case."

Again the voice stopped. Don unwrapped something that looked like a flat cigarette case with two appendages, one a disk of perforated hard rubber the size of a half dollar, and the other a three-quarter-inch-wide ribbon of opaque plastic. "I've got it, sir."

"Good. What you see is a highly advanced radio transmitter and receiver. You can imagine its value in the field. It's a pilot model you were bringing back from the contractor for tests here. But this seems as useful a way to test it as any other."

"It's range is fantastic, Captain—if you're in Washington."

"I am. Now. The key also unlocks the handcuff. Unlock it. Strip to the waist. Bend the plastic strip to fit over your shoulder—either one, as you choose. Arrange the perforated disk so it's at the base of your neck, under your shirt collar. The thing that looks like a cigarette case is the power pack."

Don followed the instructions, rubbing his wrist in relief as the handcuff came off. The radio had been well designed and its components went into place as if they had been built to his measure. They tickled a little on his bare skin, that was all. The power pack was surprisingly light.

"That's done, sir," Don said.

The answer came softly. "So I hear. You almost blasted my ear off. From now on, when you speak to me, or whoever's at this end, a barely audible murmur will be sufficient. Try it."

"Yes, Captain," Don whispered. "I'm trying it now."

"Don't whisper. I can hear you all right, but so could people you wouldn't want overhearing at your end. A whisper carries farther than you think. Talk low."

Don practiced while he put his shirt, tie and coat back on.

"Good," Captain Simmons said. "Practice talking without moving your lips, for occasions when you might have to transmit to us in someone's view. Now put your handcuff back on and lock it."

"Oh, damn," Don said under his breath.

"I heard that."

"Sorry, sir, but it is a nuisance."

"I know, but you have to get rid of it logically. When you get a chance go to the local bank. It's the Superior State Bank on McEntee Street. Show them your credentials from Riggs National and ask them to keep your brief case in their vault. Get a receipt. Then, at your first opportunity, burn the plastic key and your ID card."

"Yes, sir."

"Keep up your masquerade as a bank messenger and try to find out, as if you were an ordinary curiosity-seeker, all you can about Cavalier Institute. You've made a good start with the Garet girl. Get to know her father, the professor."

"Yes, sir." Don realized with embarrassment that his little romantic interlude with Alis must have been eavesdropped on. "Are there any particular times I'm to report?"

"You will be reporting constantly. That's the beauty of this radio."

"You mean I can't turn it off? I won't have any privacy? There'll always be somebody listening?"

"Exactly. But you mustn't be inhibited. Your private life is still your own and no one will criticize. Your unofficial actions will simply be ignored."

"Oh, great!"

"You must rely on our discretion, Sergeant. I'm sure you'll get used to it. Enough of this for now. We mustn't excite Clark's suspicions. Go back to him now and carry on. You'll receive further instructions as they are necessary. And remember—don't be inhibited."

"No, sir," Don said ruefully. He went back to the printshop, feeling like a goldfish bowl.

CHAPTER FOUR

Ed Clark took Don to the Superior State Bank and introduced him to the president, who was delighted to do business with a representative of Riggs National of Washington, D. C. Don told him nothing about the contents of the brief case, but the banker seemed to be under the impression they were securities or maybe even a million dollars cash, and Don said nothing to spoil his pleasure.

Outside again, with the receipt in his wallet, Don stood with Clark on the corner of McEntee Street and Broadway.

"This is the heart of town, you might say," the newspaper editor said. "The bubble gum factory is over that way, on the railroad spur. Maybe you can smell it. Smells real nice, I think."

Don rubbed the wrist that had been manacled for so long. He was sniffing politely when there was a roar of engines and a squadron of fighter planes buzzed Broadway.

They screamed over at little more than roof level, then were gone. They were overhead so briefly that Don noticed only that they were P-38's, at least four of them.

"Things are beginning to happen," Don said. "The Air Force is having a look-see."

Clark shook his head. "That wasn't the Air Force. Those were the PP boys. They're the only ones who fly those Lightnings these days."

"PP?"

"Private Pilots. Bobby the Bold's airborne vigilantes. Wonder what they're up to?"

"Oh. Senator Bobby Thebold, S.O.B."

"If you want to put it that way, yes."

"It's a private joke. But I think I know what they're up to—or why. The Senator's secretary is marooned up here, like me. She was on the train, too."

"You don't say! I got scooped on that one. Which one is she?"

"The redhead. Geneva Jervis. I haven't seen her since last night, come to think of it."

The P-38's screamed over again, this time from west to east. Don counted six planes now and made out the PP markings. People had come out of stores and business buildings and were looking out of upstairs windows at the sky. They were rewarded by a third thundering flypast of the fighter planes. They were higher this time, spread out laterally as if to search maximum terrain.

"Big deal," Clark said. "This show would bring anyone outdoors, but even if they see her what do you suppose they can do about it? There's no place in town flat enough for a Piper Cub to land, let alone a fighter plane."

"How about the golf course?"

"Raleigh? Worst set of links in the whole United States. A helicopter could put down there, but that's about all. What's old Bobby so worked up about, I wonder? Unless there's something to that gossip about this Jervis girl being his mistress and he's showing off for her."

"He'd show off for anybody, they tell me," Don said. Then he remembered that Military Intelligence was listening in. If any pro-Thebold people were among his eavesdroppers, he hoped they respected his private right to be anti-Thebold.

At that moment he and Clark were thrown against the side of the bank building. They clung to each other and Don noticed that the sun had moved a few degrees in the sky.

"Oh-oh," Clark grunted. "Superior's taking evasive action. Thinks it's being attacked." As they regained their footing he asked, "Do you feel heavy in the legs?"

"Yes. As if I were going up in an express elevator."

"Exactly. Somebody's getting us up beyond the reach of these pesky planes, I'd guess."

The P-38's were overhead again, but now they seemed to be diving on the town. More likely, if Clark's theory was right, it was an illusion—the planes were flying level but the town was rising fast.

"They'd better climb," Don said, "or they'll crash!"

There was the sound of a crash almost immediately, from the south end of town. Don and Clark ran toward it, fighting the heaviness in their legs.

A dozen others were ahead of them, running sluggishly across South Creek Bridge. Beyond, just short of the edge, was the wreckage of a fighter plane and, behind it, the torn-up ground of a crash landing. There was no fire.

The pilot struggled out of the cockpit. He dropped to the ground, felt himself to see if any bones were broken, then saw the crowd running toward him.

The pilot hesitated, then ran toward the edge. Shouts came from the crowd. With a last glance over his shoulder, the pilot leaped and went over the edge.

The crowd, Don and Clark among them, approached more cautiously. They made out a falling dot and, a second later, saw a parachute blossom open. The other planes appeared and flew a wide protective circle around the chutist.

"Do you think that's Bobby Thebold?" Don asked.

"Probably not. That was the last plane in the formation. Thebold would be the leader."

They went back past the crashed plane, surrounded by a growing crowd from town, and recrossed the bridge.

"Look at the water," the editor said. "Ice is forming."

"And we're still rising," Don said, "if my legs are any judge. Do you think there's a connection?"

Clark shrugged. He turned up his coat collar and rubbed his hands. "All I know is the higher we go the colder we get. Come on back to the shop and warm up."

They turned at the sound of engines. Two of the five remaining P-38's had detached themselves from their cover of the chutist and were flying around the rim of Superior—as if unwilling to risk another flight across the surface of the town that seemed determined to become a satellite of Earth.

When Don Cort reached the campus he was shivering, in spite of the sweater and topcoat Ed Clark had lent him. He asked a student where the Administration Building was and at the desk inquired for Professor Garet.

A gray-haired, dedicated-looking woman told him impatiently that Professor Garet was in his laboratory and couldn't be disturbed. She wouldn't tell him where the laboratory was.

"Have you seen Miss Jervis?" Don wondered whether the redhead appreciated the demonstration her boss, the flying Senator, had put on for her.

The woman behind the desk shook her head. "You're two of the people from the train, aren't you? Well, you're all supposed to report to the dining room at two o'clock."

"What for?"

"You'll find out at two o'clock."

It was obvious he would get no more information from her. Don left the building. It was half-past one. He crossed the near-deserted campus. His legs still felt heavy and he assumed Superior was still rising. It certainly seemed to be getting increasingly colder.

He wondered how high they were and whether it would snow. He hoped not. How high did you have to be before

110

you got up where it didn't snow any more? He had no idea. He did recall that Mount Everest was 29,000 feet up and that it snowed up there. Or would it be *down* there, relatively speaking? How high could they be, and didn't anybody care?

The frosty old receptionist seemed to be typical in her business-as-usual, come-what-may attitude. Even Ed Clark didn't seem as concerned as he ought to be about Superior's ascent into the stratosphere. Clark was interested, certainly, but he'd given Don the impression that he was no more curious than he would be about any other phenomenon he'd write about in next week's paper—a two-headed calf, for instance.

Don remembered now that the conquerors of Everest had needed oxygen in the rarefied atmosphere near the summit and he experimentally took a couple of deep breaths. No difficulty. Therefore they weren't 29,000 feet up—yet. Small comfort, he thought, as he shivered again.

He picked out a building at random. Classes were in session behind the closed but windowed doors along the hall. From the third door he saw Alis Garet, sitting at the back of a small classroom. Her attention had wandered from the instructor and when she saw Don she smiled and beckoned. He hesitated, then opened the door and went in as quietly as he could. The instructor paused briefly, nodded, then went back to a droning lecture. It seemed to be an English literature class.

Alis cleared some books off a chair next to her and Don sat down. "Who turned you loose?" she whispered.

He realized she was referring to his de-handcuffed wrist and grinned, indicating that he'd tell her later.

"I see you've been outfitted for our new climate," she went on. A student in the row of chairs ahead turned and frowned. The instructor talked on, oblivious.

Don nodded and said "*Sh.*"

"Don't let them intimidate you. Did you see the planes?"

More students were turning and glaring and Don's embarrassment grew. "Come on," he said. "Let's cut this class."

"Bravo!" she said. "Spoken like a true Cavalier."

She gathered up her books. The instructor, without interrupting his lecture, followed them with his eyes as they left the room.

"Now I'll never know whether the young princes got out of the tower alive," she said.

"They didn't. The question is, will we?"

"I certainly hope so. I'll have to speak to Father about it."

"He's locked up in his lab, they tell me. Where would that be?"

"In the tower, as a matter of fact. The bell tower that the founding fathers built and then didn't have enough money to buy bells for. But you can't go up there—it's the holy of holies."

"Can you?"

"No. Why? You don't think Father is making all this happen, do you?"

"Somebody is. Professor Garet seems as good a suspect as any."

"Oh, he likes to act mysterious, but it's all an act. Poor old Father is just a crackpot theorist. I told you that. He couldn't pick up steel filing with a magnet."

"I wonder. Look, somebody's called a meeting for us outsiders from the train at two o'clock. It's almost that now. Maybe I'll have a chance to ask some questions. Will your father be there?"

"I'm sure he will. He's a great meeting-caller. I'll go with you. And, since you have two free hands now, you can hold my books. Maybe later you'll get a chance to hold me."

Among the people sitting around the bare tables in the dining room, Don recognized the conductor and other trainmen, two stocky individuals who had the look of traveling salesmen, an elderly couple who held hands, a young couple with a baby, two nuns, a soldier apparently going on or returning from furlough, and a tall, hawk-nosed man Don classified on no evidence at all as a Shakespearean actor. All had been on the train. He didn't see Geneva Jervis anywhere.

An improvised speaker's table had been set up at one end of the room, near the door to the kitchen. A heavy-set man sat at the table talking to Mrs. Garet, the professor's wife.

"The stoutish gentleman next to Mother is the president of Cavalier," Alis said. "Maynard Rubach. When you talk to him be sure to call him *Doctor* Rubach. He's not a Ph.D. and he's sensitive about it, but he did used to be a veterinarian."

They sat down near the big table and Mrs. Garet smiled and waved at them. Mayor Civek came in through the kitchen door, licking a finger as if he'd been sampling something on the way, and sat down next to Mrs. Garet.

At that moment Don's stomach gave a hop and he felt blood rushing to his head. Others also had pained or nauseous expressions.

"Ugh," Alis said. "Now what?"

"I'd guess," Don said when his stomach had settled back in place, "that we've stopped rising."

"You mean we've gone as high as we're going to go?"

"I hope so. We'd run out of air if we went much higher."

Professor Garet came in presently, looking pleased with himself. He nodded to his wife and the men next to her and cleared his throat as he looked out over the room.

"Altitude 21,500 feet," he announced without preamble. "Temperature sixteen degrees Fahrenheit. From here on out—" he paused, repeated "out" and chuckled. "It's going to be a bit chilly. Those of you who are inadequately clothed will see my wife for extra garments. I believe you have been comfortably housed and fed. There will, of course, be no charge for these services while you are the guests of the Cavalier Institute of Applied Sciences. Thank you. I now present Mr. Hector Civek, the mayor of Superior, who will answer any other questions you may have."

Don looked at Alis, who shrugged. The conductor stood and opened a notebook which he consulted. "I have a few questions, Mr. Mayor. These people have asked me to speak for them and there's one question that outweighs all the others. That is—are you going to take us back to Earth? If so, when? And how?"

Civek cleared his throat. He took a sip of water. "As for the first question—we certainly hope to take you and ourselves back to Earth. I can't answer the others."

"You hope to?"

"Earnestly. I turn blue easily myself, and I'm as anxious as you are to get back. But when that will be depends entirely on circumstances. Circumstances, uh, beyond my control."

"Who's controlling them, then? Your friend with the whiskers?"

Professor Garet smiled amiably and patted his beard. The portly Maynard Rubach got up and Civek sat down.

"I am Dr. Maynard Rubach, president of Cavalier. I must insist that in common decency we all refrain from personal references. Mr. Civek has done his best to give you an explanation, but of course he is a layman and, while he has many excellent qualities, we cannot expect him to be conversant with the principles of science. I will therefore attempt to explain.

"As you know, science has been aware for hundreds of years that the Earth is a giant magnet..."

Don saw Geneva Jervis. She was at the kitchen door beyond the speaker's table.

"...the isogenic and the isoclinic..."

The red-haired Miss Jervis saw Don now and put her finger to her lips.

"...an ultimote, which is simultaneously an integral part of..."

Now the redhead was beckoning to him urgently. He excused himself to Alis, who frowned when she saw the other girl; then he went back of the speaker's table ("...1,257 tenescopes to the square centimeter...") into the kitchen. Jen Jervis was now at the far end of it motioning him to hurry up.

"I've found something," she said. She was wearing a shapeless fur coat, apparently borrowed.

"Come on. You'll have to see it."

"All right, but why me?"

"Aside from myself you seem to be the only one from the train with any gumption. I know you've been spying around doing things while everybody else sat back and waited for deliverance. Though I can't say I admire your choice of companions. That tawdry blonde—"

"Now, really, Miss Jervis!"

"Tawny, then; sometimes I mix up my words."

"I'll bet."

She led him out the back door and past several buildings. They reached what once must have been an athletic field.

"At the far end," she said. "Come on."

"Where were you when your boy friend and his daredevil aces came over?"

"I saw them."

"Did they see you?"

"None of your business."

He shrugged. They were at a section of the grandstand at the end of the field. Jen Jervis indicated a door and Don opened it. It led to a big room under the stands. "What does this remind you of?" she asked.

Don looked blank. In the dim light he could see some planking, a long-deflated football, ancient peanut shells and an empty pint bottle. "I don't know. What?"

"Stagg Field? At the University of Chicago? Under the stands where they first made an atomic pile work?" She looked at him with the air of an investigator hot on the scent.

He shrugged. "Never been there. So what?"

"It's a pattern. This is where they've hidden their secret."

"It looks more like the place a co-ed and her boy friend might go to have a little fun. In warmer weather, of course."

"Oh!" she said. "You're disgusting! Look over there."

He looked, wondering what made this young attractive woman hypersensitive on the subject of sex. This was the second time she'd blazed up over nothing. What he saw where she pointed was a door at a 45-degree angle to the ground, set into a triangular block of concrete. "Where does that go?" he asked.

"Down," she said as they walked toward it. "And there's some machinery or something down there. I heard it. Or maybe I only felt the vibrations. It throbs, anyway."

"Probably the generator for the school's lighting system. Did you go down and look?"

"No."

"All right, then." He opened the door. "Down we go."

At the bottom of a flight of steps there was a corridor lit by dim electric light bulbs along one wall. The corridor became a tunnel, sloping gradually downward. They had been going north, Don judged, but then the tunnel made a right turn and now they were following it due east. "I don't hear any throbbing," he said.

"Well, I did, and from way up here. They must have turned it off."

"How long ago was that?"

"An hour, maybe."

"While we were still rising. That would make sense. We've stopped again, you know. Professor Garet gave us a bulletin on it."

He had been going ahead of her in the narrow tunnel. Now it widened and they were able to walk side by side. There seemed to be no end to it. But then they came to a sturdy-looking door, padlocked.

"That's that," Don said.

"That's that nothing," she said. "Break it down."

He laughed. "You flatter me. Come on back."

"Don't you think this is at all peculiar? A tunnel starting under an abandoned grandstand, running all this way and ending in a locked door?"

"Maybe this was a station on the underground railway. It looks old enough."

"We're going through that door." She opened her purse and took out a key ring. On it was an extensive collection of keys. Eventually she found one that opened the padlock.

"Well!" he said. "Who taught you *that*?"

"Open the door."

The corridor beyond the door was lined—walls, ceiling and floor—with a silvery metal. It continued east a hundred yards or so, swung north and then went east again, widening all the time.

It ended in a great room whose far wall was glass or some equally transparent substance. The room was a huge observatory at the end of Superior but below its rim. They could look down from it, not without a touch of nausea, to the Earth four miles below.

Don, thinking of the surface of Superior above, thought it was as if they were looking out of the gondola slung beneath a dirigible.

Or from one of the lower portholes in a giant flying saucer.

CHAPTER FIVE

There were clouds below that occasionally hid the Earth from sight. For a minute or more they gazed in silence at the magnificent view.

"This wasn't built in a day," Jen Jervis said at last.

"I should say not," Don agreed. "Millions of years."

She looked at him sharply. "I wasn't talking about the age of the Earth. I mean this room—this lookout post—whatever it is."

He grinned at her. "I agree with you there, too. I'm really a very agreeable fellow, Miss Jervis. Obviously, whoever built it knew well in advance that Superior was going to take off. They also knew how much of it was going up and exactly where this would have to be built so it would be at the edge."

"Under the edge, you mean, with a downward view."

"That's right. From a distance I'd say Superior looked as if someone had cut the end off an orange. The flat part—where the cut was made—is the surface and we're looking out from a piece of the convex skin."

"You put things so simply, Mr. Cort, that even a child could understand," she said acidly.

"Thank you," he said complacently. He had remembered that whoever was listening in for Military Intelligence through the tiny radio under his shirt could have only a vague idea of what was going on. Any little word pictures he could supply, therefore, would help them understand. He had to risk the fact that his companion might think him a bit of an idiot.

Of course with this Geneva Jervis it was easy to lay himself open to the scathing comment and the barbed retort.

He imagined she was extremely useful in her role as Girl Friday to Senator Bobby Thebold.

"I don't think this is the work of those boobies at the booby hatch," she was saying.

"I beg your pardon?"

"The Cavalier Institution of Applied Foolishness, whatever they call it. They just wouldn't be capable of an undertaking of this scope."

"Oh, I agree. That's why I let you drag me away from the meeting. It was a lot of pseudo-scientific malarkey. Old Doc Rubach, D.V.M., was going on about the ultimote being connected to the thighbone, way up in the middle of the air. Tell me, who do *you* think is behind it all?"

She was walking around the big-sided room as if taking mental inventory. There wasn't much to catalogue—six straight chairs, heavy and modern-looking, with a large wooden table, a framed piece of dark glass that might be a television set, and a gray steel box about the size and shape of a three-drawer filing cabinet. This last was near the big window-wall and had three black buttons on its otherwise smooth top. Don itched to push the buttons to see what would happen. Jen Jervis seemed to have the same urge. She drummed on the box with her long fingernails.

"I?" she said. "Behind it all?"

"Yes. What's your theory? Is this something for the Un-Earthly Activities Committee to investigate?"

"Don't be impertinent. If the Senator thinks it's his duty to look into it, he will. He undoubtedly is already. In the meantime, I can do no less than gather whatever information I can while I'm on the scene."

"Very patriotic. What do you conclude from your information-gathering so far?"

"Obviously there's some kind of conspiracy—" she began, then stopped as if she suspected a trap.

"—afoot," Don said with a grin. "As I see it, all you do is have Bobby the Bold subpoena everybody up here—every last man-jack of 'em—to testify before his committee. They wouldn't dare refuse."

"I don't find you a bit amusing, Mr. Cort, though I have no doubt this sophomoric humor makes a big hit with your teen-age blonde. We'd better get back. I can see it was a mistake to expect any co-operation from you."

"As you like, Madame Investigator." Don gave her a mock bow, then turned for a last look down at the vast segment of Earth below.

Geneva Jervis screamed.

He whirled to see her standing, big-eyed and open-mouthed, in front of the framed dark glass he had taken for a television screen. Her face was contorted in horror, and as Don's gaze flicked to the screen he had the barest glimpse of a pair of eyes fading with a dissolving image. Then the screen was blank and Don wasn't sure whether there had been a face to go with the eyes—an inhuman, un-earthly face—or whether his imagination had supplied it.

The girl slumped to the floor in a faint.

COLUMBUS, OHIO, Nov. 1 (AP)—Sen. Robert (Bobby) Thebold landed here today after leading his Private Pilots (PP) squadron of P-38's on a reconnaissance flight which resulted in the loss of one of the six World War II fighters in a crash landing on the mysteriously airborne town of Superior, Ohio. The pilot of the crashed plane parachuted safely to Earth.

Sen. Thebold told reporters grimly:

"There is no doubt in my mind that mysterious forces are at work when a town of 3,000 population can rise in a body off the face of the Earth. My reconnaissance has shown conclusively that the town is intact and its inhabitants alive. On one of my passes I saw my secretary, Miss Geneva Jervis."

Sen. Thebold said he was confident Miss Jervis would contact him the moment she had anything to report, indicating she would make an on-the-spot investigation.

The Senator said in reply to a question that he was "amazed" at official Washington's "complete inaction" in the matter, and declared he would demand a probe by the Senate Investigations Subcommittee, of which he is a member. He indicated witnesses might include officials of the Defense Department, the Central Intelligence Agency, and "possibly others."

LADENBURG, Ohio, Nov. 1 (UPI)—Little Ladenburg, former neighbor of "The City in the Sky," complained today of a rain of empty beer cans and other rubbish, apparently being tossed over the edge by residents of airborne Superior.

"They're not so high and mighty," one sanitation official here said, "that they can make Ladenburg their garbage dump."

WASHINGTON, Nov. 1 (Reuters)—American officials today were at a loss to explain the strange behaviour of Superior, Ohio, "the town that took off."

Authoritative sources assured Reuters that no military or scientific experiments were in progress which could account for the phenomenon of a town being lifted intact thousands of feet into the air.

Rumors circulating to the effect that a "Communist plot" was at work were greeted with extreme scepticism in official quarters.

Bulletin
COLUMBUS, Ohio, Nov. 1 (UPI)—The airborne town of Superior began to drift east across Ohio late today.

CHAPTER SIX

The unconscious Geneva Jervis, lying crumpled up in the oversized fur coat, was the immediate problem. Don Cort straightened her out so she lay on her back, took off her shoes and propped her ankles on the lower rung of a chair. He found she was wearing a belt and loosened it. It was obvious that she was also wearing a girdle but there wasn't anything he wanted to do about that. He was rubbing one of her wrists when her eyes fluttered open.

She smiled self-consciously. "I guess I was a sissy."

"Not at all. I saw it, too. A pair of eyes."

"And a face! A horrible, horrible face."

"I wasn't sure about the face. Can you describe it?"

She darted a tentative look at the screen but it was comfortingly blank. "It wasn't human. And it was staring right into me. It was awful!"

"Did it have a nose, ears, mouth?"

"I—I can't be sure. Let's get out of here. I'm all right now. Thanks for being so good to me—Don."

"Don't mention it—Jen. Here, put your shoes on."

When he had closed the big wooden door behind them, Don padlocked it again. He preferred to leave things as they'd found them, even though their visit to the observation room was no longer a secret.

He was relieved when they had scrambled up the steps under the grandstand. There had been no sense of anyone or anything following them or spying on them during their long walk through the tunnel.

They were silent with their separate thoughts as they crossed the frosty ground and Jen held Don's arm, more for companionship than support. At the campus the girl excused herself, saying she still felt shaky and wanted to rest in her room. Don went back to the dining room.

The meeting was over but Alis Garet was there, having a cup of tea and reading a book.

"Well, sir," she said, giving him an intent look, "how was the rendezvous?"

"Fair to middling." He was relieved to see that she wasn't angry. "Did anybody say anything while I was gone?"

"Not a coherent word. You don't deserve it but I made notes for you. Running off with that redhead when you have a perfectly adequate blonde. Did you kiss her?"

"Of course not. It was strictly business. Let me see the notes, you angel."

"Notes, then." She handed over a wad of paper.

"Rubach," he read, "Magnology stuff stuff stuff etc. etc. Nothing.

"Q.   (Conductor Jas Brown) Wht abt Mayor's proclamation Superior seceded frm Earth?

"A. (Civek) Repeated stuff abt discrimination agnst Spr & Cavlr & bubl gum prices.

"Q. Wht u xpct gain?

"A. Stuff abt end discrimination.

"Q. Sovereignty?

"A. How's that?

"Q. R u trying set up Spr as separate city-state w/govt independent of U S or Earth? ('That Conductor Brown is sharper than I gave him credit for,' Alis elaborated.)

"A. Hem & haw. Well now.

"Q. Well, r u?

"A. (Father, rescuing Civek) Q of sovereignty must remain temporarily up in the air. Laughter (Father's). When

& if Spr returns wil acpt state-fed laws as b4 but meantime circs warrant adapt to prevailing conditions.

"Rest of mtg was abt sleeping arngmnts, meals, recreation privileges, clothing etc."

Don folded the notes and put them in his pocket. "Thanks. I see I didn't miss much. The only thing it seems to add is that Mayor Civek is a figurehead, and that if the Cavalier people know anything they're not talking, except in gobbledygook."

"Check," Alis said. "Now let's go take a look at Pittsburgh."

"Pittsburgh?"

"That's where we are now. One of the students who lives there peeped over the edge a while ago. I was waiting for you to come back before I went to have a look."

"Pittsburgh?" Don repeated. "You mean Superior's drifting across the United States?"

"Either that or it's being pushed. Let's go see."

There hadn't been much to see and it had been too cold to watch for long. The lights of Pittsburgh were beginning to go on in the dusk and the city looked pretty and far away. A Pennsylvania Air National Guard plane came up to investigate, but from a respectful distance. Then it flew off.

Don left Alis, shivering, at her door and decided he wanted a drink. He remembered having seen a sign, *Club Lyric*, down the street from the *Sentry* office and he headed for it.

"Sergeant Cort," said a muffled voice under his collar.

Don jumped. He'd forgotten for the moment that he was a walking radio station. "Yes?" he said.

"Reception has been excellent," the voice said. It was no longer that of Captain Simmons. "You needn't recapitulate. We've heard all your conversations and feel we know as much as you do. You'll have to admit it isn't much."

"I'm afraid not. What do you want me to do now? Should I go back and investigate that underground room again? That seems to be the best lead so far."

"No. You're just a bank messenger whose biggest concern was to safeguard the contents of the brief case. Now that the contents are presumably in the bank vault your official worries are over, and though you're curious to know why Superior's acting the way it is, you're willing to let somebody else do something about it."

"But they saw me in the room. Those eyes, whatever they are. I had the feeling—well, that they weren't human."

"Nonsense!" the voice from the Pentagon said. "An ordinary closed-circuit television hookup. Don't let your imagination run away with you, and above all don't play spy. If they're suspicious of anyone it will be of Geneva Jervis because of her connection with Senator Thebold. Where are you going now?"

"Well, sir, I thought—that is, if there's no objection—I thought I'd go have a drink. See what the townspeople are saying."

"Good idea. Do that."

"What are they saying in Washington? Does anybody put any stock in this magnology stuff of Professor Garet's?"

"Facts are being collated. There's been no evaluation yet. You'll hear from us again when there's something to tell you. For now, Cort, carry on. You're doing a splendid job."

The streets were cold, dark, and deserted. The few street lights were feeble and the lights in houses and other buildings seemed dimmer than normal. A biting wind had sprung up and Don was glad when he saw the neon words *Club Lyric* ahead.

The bartender greeted him cheerfully. "It ain't a fit night. What'll it be?"

Don decided on a straight shot, to start. "What's going on?" he asked. "Where's the old town going?"

The bartender shrugged. "Let Civek worry about that. It's what we pay him for, ain't it?"

"I suppose so. How're you fixed for liquor? Big supply?"

"Last a coupla weeks unless people start drinking more than usual. Beer'll run out first."

"That's right, I guess. But aren't you worried about being up in the air like this?"

The bartender shrugged again. "Not much I can do about it, is there? Want another shot?"

"Mix it this time. A little soda. Is that the general attitude? Business as usual?"

"I hear some business is picking up. Lot of people buying winter clothes, for one thing, weather turning cold the way it did. And Dabney Brothers—they run the coal and fuel oil company—got enough orders to keep them going night and day for a week."

"That's fine. But when they eventually run out, like you, then what? Everybody freeze to death?"

The bartender made a thoughtful face. "You got something there. Oh, hello, Ed. Kinda brisk tonight."

It was Ed Clark, the newspaperman. Clark nodded to the bartender, who began to mix him a martini. "Freeze the ears off a brass monkey," Clark said, joining Don. "I have an extra pair of earmuffs if you'd like them."

"Thanks," Don said, "but I think I'd better buy myself some winter clothes tomorrow and return yours."

"Suit yourself. Planning to settle down here?"

"I don't seem to have much choice. Anything new at your end?"

Clark lifted his brimming glass and took a sip. "Here's to a mild winter. New? I guess you know we're in Pennsylvania now and not Ohio. *Over* Pennsylvania, I should say. Don't ask me why, unless Hector Civek thinks Superior will get a better break, taxwise."

"You think the mayor's behind it all?"

"He has his delusions of grandeur, like a lot of people here. But I do think Hector knows more than he's telling. Some of the merchants—mostly those whose business hasn't benefited by the cold wave—have called a meeting for tomorrow. They want to pump him."

"He wasn't exactly a flowing spout at Cavalier this afternoon when the people from the train wanted answers."

"So that's where he was. They couldn't find him at Town Hall."

"Where's it all going to end? If we keep on drifting we'll be over the Atlantic—next stop Europe. Then Superior will be crossing national boundaries instead of just state lines, and some country may decide we're violating its air space and shoot us out of the sky."

"I see you take the long view," Clark said.

"Is there any other?" Don asked. "The alternative is to kid ourselves that everything's all right and trust in Providence and Hector Civek. What is it with you people? You don't seem to realize that sixteen square miles of solid earth, and three thousand people, have taken off to go waltzing through the sky. That isn't just something that happens. Something or somebody's making it happen. The question is who or what, and what are you going to do about it?"

The bartender said, "The boy's right, Ed. How do we know they won't take us up higher—up where there's no air? Then we'd be cooked."

Clark laughed. "'Cooked' is hardly the word. But I agree that things are getting out of hand." He set down his glass with a clink. "I know the man we want. Old Doc Bendy. He could stir things up. Remember the time they tried to run the pipeline through town and Doc formed a citizens committee and stopped them?"

"Stopped them dead," the bartender recalled, then cleared his throat. "Speak of the devil." He raised his voice and greeted the man who had just walked in. "Well, Doc. Long time since we've had the pleasure of your company. Nice to see you."

Doc Bendy was an imposing old gentleman of more than average height and magnificent girth. He carried a paunch with authority. His hands, at the ends of short arms, seemed to fall naturally to it, and he patted the paunch with satisfaction as he spoke. He was dressed for the cold weather in an old frock coat, black turning green, with a double line of oversized buttons down the front and huge eighteenth-century lapels. He wore a battered black slouch hat which long ago had given up the pretense of holding any particular shape.

"Salutations, gentlemen!" Doc Bendy boomed, striding majestically toward the bar. "They tell me our peripatetic little town has just passed Pittsburgh. I'd have thought it more likely we'd crossed the Arctic Circle. Rum, bartender, is the only suitable potable for the occasion."

Clark introduced Don, who saw that close up Doc Bendy's face was full and firm rather than fat. The nose had begun to develop the network of visible blood vessels which indicated a fondness for the bottle. Shaggy white eyebrows matched the fringe of white hair that sprouted from under the sides and back of the slouch hat. The eyes themselves were alert and humorous. The mouth rose subtly at the corners and, though Bendy never seemed to smile outright, it conveyed the same humor as the eyes. These two features, in fact, saved the old man from seeming pompous.

Don noticed that the rum the bartender poured for Bendy was 151 proof and the portion was a generous one.

Bendy raised his glass. "Your health, gentlemen." He took a sip and put it down. "I might also drink to a happy voyage, destination unknown."

"Don here thinks we're in danger of drifting over Europe."

"A distinct possibility," Bendy said. "Your passports are in order, I trust? I remember the first time I went to the Continent. It was with Black Jack Pershing and the AEF."

"Were you in the Medical Corps, sir?" Don asked.

Doc Bendy boomed with laughter, holding his paunch. "Bless your soul, lad, I'm no doctor. I was on the board of directors of Superior's first hospital, hence the title. A mere courtesy, conferred on me by a grateful citizenry."

"The citizens might be looking to you again, Doc," Clark said, "since their elected representatives are letting them down."

"But not *bringing* them down, eh? Suppose you tell me what you know, Mr. Editor. I assume you're the best-informed man on the situation, barring the conspirators who have dragged us aloft."

"You think it's a conspiracy?"

"It's not an act of God."

Clark began to fill an ancient pipe, so well caked that the pencil with which he tamped the tobacco barely fitted into the bowl. By the time the pipe was ready for a match he had exhausted the solid facts. Don then took over and described the underground passage he had seen that afternoon. He was about to go further when the old man held up a hand.

"The facts only, if you please. Mr. Cort, what you saw in the underground chamber fits in remarkably with something I stumbled on this afternoon while I was skating."

"Skating?" Clark said.

"Ice skating. At North Lake. It's completely frozen over and I'm not so decrepit that I can't glide on a pair of blades. Well, I was gliding along, humming the *Skater's Waltz*, when I tripped over a stump. When I said I stumbled on something I was speaking literally, because I fell flat. While I lay there, with the breath knocked out of me, my face was only an inch from the ice and I realized I was eye-to-eye with a thing. Just as you were, Mr. Cort."

"You mean there was something under the ice?"

"Exactly. Staring up at me. Balefully, I suppose you could say, as if it resented my presence."

"Did you see the whole face?"

"I'd be embroidering if I said yes. It seemed—but I must stick to the facts. I saw only the eyes. Two perfectly circular eyes, which glared at me for a moment, then disappeared."

"It could have been a fish," Clark said.

"No. A fish is about the most expressionless thing there is, while these eyes had intelligence behind them. None of your empty, fishy stares."

Clark knocked his pipe against the edge of the bar so the ashes fell in the vicinity of an old brass cuspidor. "So, since what you and Don saw were both under the surface, we could put two and two together and assume that some kind of alien beings have taken up residence in Superior's lower levels?"

"Only if you think two and two make five," Doc Bendy said. "But even if they don't, there's a great deal more going on than Civek knows, or the Garet-Rubach crowd at Cavalier will admit. It seems to me, gentlemen, that it's time I set up a committee."

CHAPTER SEVEN

Miss Leora Frisbie, spinster, was found dead in the mushroom cellar of her home on Ryder Avenue in the northeastern part of town. She had been sitting in a camp chair, bundled in heavy clothing, when she died. She had been subject to heart trouble and that fact, coupled with notes she had been making on a pad in her lap, led the coroner to believe she had been frightened to death.

The first entry on the pad said: *Someone stealing my mushrooms; must keep vigil.* The notes continued:

Sitting in chair near stairs. Single 60-w. bulb dims, gravity increases. Superior rising again? Movement in corner—soil being pushed up from underneath. Hand. Hand? Claw!

Claw withdraws.

Head. Rat? No. Bigger.

Human? No. But the eyes eyes ey

That was all.

Photostatic copies of the late Miss Frisbie's notes and the coroner's report became exhibits one and two in Doc Bendy's dossier. Exhibit three was a carbon copy of a report by the stock control clerk at the bubble gum factory.

Bubble gum had been piling up in the warehouse on the railroad siding back of Reilly Street. The stock control clerk, Armand Specht, was taking inventory when he saw a movement at the far end of the warehouse. His report follows:

Investigated and found carton had been dislodged from top of pile and broken into. Gross of Cheeky brand missing. Saw something sitting with back to me opening packages, stuffing gum into mouth, wax paper and all, half-dozen at time. Looked like overgrown chimpanzee. It turned and saw me, continuing to chew. Didn't get clear look before it disappeared but noticed two things: one, that its cheeks bulged out from chewing so much gum at once, and other, that its eyes were round and bright, even in dim corner. Then animal turned and disappeared behind pile of Cheekys. No chimpanzee. Didn't follow right away but when I did it was gone.

Exhibit four:

Dear Diary:

There wasn't any TV tonight and I asked Grandfather Bendy what to do and he said "Marie, when I was young, boys and girls made their own fun" and so I got out the Scrabble and asked Mom and Dad to play but they said no they had to go to the Warners and play bridge. So they went and I was playing pretending I was both sides when the door opened and I said Hello Grandfather but it wasn't him it was like a kangaroo and it had big eyes that were friendly.

After a while I went over and scratched its ears and it liked that and then it went over to the table and looked at the Scrabble. I thought wouldn't it be funny if it could play but it couldn't. But it could spell! It had hands like claws with long black fingernails and fur on them (the fingers) and it pushed the letters around so they spelled Name and I spelled out Marie.

Then I spelled out Who are you and it spelled Gizl.

Then I spelled How old are you and it put all the blank spaces together.

I said Where do you live and it spelled Here. Then I changed to Where do you come from and it pointed to the blanks again.

The gizl went away before Mom and Dad came home and I didn't tell them about it but I'll tell Grandfather Bendy because he understands better about things like the time I had an invisible friend.

Don Cort went to bed in the dormitory at Cavalier with the surprised realization that it had been only twenty-four hours since Superior took off. It seemed more like a week. When he woke up the floating town was over New York.

Some high-flying skywriters were at work. *Welcome Superior—Drink Pepsi-Cola* their message said.

Don dressed quickly and hurried to the brink. Alis Garet was there among a little crowd, bundled up in a parka.

"Is that the Hudson River?" she asked him. "Where's the Empire State Building?"

"Yes," he said. "Haven't you ever been to New York? I can't quite make it out. It's somewhere south of that patch of green—that's Central Park."

"No, I've never been out of Ohio. I thought New York was a big city."

"It's big enough. Don't forget we're four miles up. Have you seen any planes besides the skywriters?"

"Just some airliners, way down," she said. "Were you expecting someone?"

"Seeing how it's our last port of call, I thought there might be some Federal boys flying around. I shouldn't think they'd want a chunk of their real estate exported to Europe."

"Are we going to Europe?"

"Bound to if we don't change course."

"Why?"

"My very next words were going to be 'Don't ask me why.' I ask you. You're closer to the horse's mouth than I am."

"If you mean Father," Alis said, "I told you I don't enjoy his confidence."

"Haven't you even got an inkling of what he's up to?"

"I'm sure he's not the Master Mind, if that's what you mean."

"Then who is? Rubach? Civek? The chief of police? Or the bubble gum king, whoever he is?"

"Cheeky McFerson?" She laughed. "I went to grade school with him and if he's got a mind I never noticed it."

"McFerson? He's just a kid, isn't he?"

"His father died a couple of years ago and Cheeky's the president on paper, but the business office runs things. We call him Cheeky because he always had a wad of company gum in his cheek. Supposed to be an advertisement. But he never gave me any and I always chewed Wrigley's for spite."

"Oh." Don chewed the inside of his own cheek and watched the coastline. "That's Connecticut now," he said. "We're certainly not slowing down for customs."

A speck, trailing vapor through the cold upper air, headed toward them from the general direction of New England. As it came closer Don saw that it was a B-58 Hustler bomber. He recognized it by the mysterious pod it carried under its body, three-quarters as long as the fuselage.

"It's not going to shoot us down, is it?" Alis asked.

"Hardly. I'm glad to see it. It's about time somebody took an interest in us besides Bobby Thebold and his leftover Lightnings."

The B-58 rapidly closed the last few miles between them, banked and circled Superior.

"Attention people of Superior," a voice from the plane said. The magnified words reached them distinctly through the cold air. "Inasmuch as you are now leaving the continental United States, this aircraft has been assigned to accompany you. From this point on you are under the protection of the United States Air Force."

"That's better," Don said. "It's not much, but at least somebody's doing something."

The B-58 streaked off and took up a course in a vast circle around them.

"I'm not so sure I like having it around," Alis said. "I mean suppose they find out that Superior's controlled by—I don't know—let's say a foreign power, or an alien race. Once we're out over the Atlantic where nobody else could get hurt, wouldn't they maybe consider it a small sacrifice to wipe out Superior to get rid of the—the alien?"

Don looked at her closely. "What's this about an alien? What do you know?"

"I don't *know* anything. It's just a feeling I have, that this is bigger than Father and Mayor Civek and all the self-important VIP's in Superior put together." She squeezed his arm as if to draw comfort from him. "Maybe it's seeing the ocean and realizing the vastness of it, but for the first time I'm beginning to feel a little scared."

"I won't say there's nothing to be afraid of," Don said. He pulled her hand through his arm. "It isn't as though this were a precedented situation. But whatever's going on, remember there are some pretty good people on our side, too."

"I know," she said. "And you're one of them."

He wondered what she meant by that. Nothing, probably, except "Thank you for the reassurance." He decided that was it; the mechanical eavesdropper he wore under his collar was making him too self-conscious. He tried to think of something appropriate to say to her that he wouldn't mind having overheard in the Pentagon.

Nothing occurred to him, so he drew Alis closer and gave her a quick, quiet kiss.

The crowd of people looking over the edge had grown. Judging by their number, few people were in school or at their jobs today. Yesterday they had seemed only mildly interested in what their town was up to but today, with the North American continent about to be left behind, they were paying more attention. Yet Don could see no signs of alarm on their faces. At most there was a reflection of wonder, but not much more than there might be among a group of Europeans seeing New York Harbor from shipboard for the first time. An apathetic bunch, he decided, who would be resigned to their situation so long as the usual pattern of their lives was not interfered with unduly. What they lacked, of course, was leadership.

"It's big, isn't it?" Alis said. She was looking at the Atlantic, which was virtually the only thing left to see except the bright blue sky, a strip of the New England coast, and the circling bomber.

"It's going to get bigger," Don said. "Shall we go across town and take a last look at the States?" He also wanted to see what, if anything, was going on in town.

"Not the last, I hope. I'd prefer a round trip."

An enterprising cab driver opened his door for them. "Special excursion rate to the west end," he said. "One buck."

"You're on," Don said. "How's business?"

"Not what you'd call booming. No trains to meet. No buses. Hi, Alis. This isn't one of your father's brainstorms come to life, is it?"

"Hi, Chuck," she said. "I seriously doubt it, though I'm sure you'd never get him to admit it. How are your wife and the boy?"

"Fine. That boy, he's got some imagination. He's digging a hole in the back yard. Last week he told us he was getting close to China. This week it's Australia. He said at supper last night that they must have heard about this hole and started digging from the other end. They've connected up, according to him, and he had quite a conversation with a kangaroo."

"A kangaroo?" Don sat up straight.

"Yeah. You know how kids are. I guess he's studying Australia in geography."

"What did the kangaroo tell your son?"

The cab driver laughed defensively. "There's nothing wrong with the boy. He's just got an active mind."

"Of course. When I was a kid I used to talk to bears. But what did he say the kangaroo talked about?"

"Oh, just crazy stuff—like the kangaroos didn't like it Down Under any more and were coming up here because it was safer."

Later that morning, at about the time Don Cort estimated that Superior had passed the twelve-mile limit—east from the coast, not up—the Superior State Bank was held up.

A man clearly recognized as Joe Negus, a small-time gambler, and one other man had driven up to the bank in Negus' flashy Buick convertible. They walked up to the head teller, threatened him with pistols and demanded all the money in all the tills. They stuffed the bills in a sack, got into their car and drove off. They took nothing from the customers and made no attempt to take anything from the vault.

The fact that they ignored the vault made Don feel better. He thought when he first heard about the robbery that the men might have been after the brief case he'd stored there, which would have meant that he was under suspicion. But apparently the job was a genuine heist, not a cover-up for something else.

Police Chief Vincent Grande reached the scene half an hour after the criminals left it. His car had frozen up and wouldn't start. He arrived by taxi, red-faced, fingering the butt of his holstered service automatic.

Negus and his confederate, identified as a poolroom lounger named Hank Stacy, had gotten away with a hundred thousand dollars.

"I didn't know there was that much money in town," was Grande's comment on that. While he was asking other questions the telephone rang and someone told the bank president he'd seen Negus and Stacy go into the poolroom. In fact, the robbers' convertible was parked blatantly in front of the place.

Grande, looking as if he'd rather be dog catcher, got back into the taxi.

Joe Negus and Hank Stacy were sitting on opposite sides of a pool table when the police chief got there, dividing the money in three piles. A third man stood by, watching closely. He was Jerry Lynch, a lawyer. He greeted Grande.

"Morning, Vince," he said easily. "Come to shoot a little pool?"

"I'll shoot some bank robbers if they don't hand over that money," Grande said. He had his gun out and looked almost purposeful.

Negus and Stacy made no attempt to go for their guns, Stacy seemed nervous but Negus went on counting the money without looking up.

"Is it your money, Vince?" Jerry Lynch asked.

"You know damn well whose money it is. Now let's have it."

"I'm afraid I couldn't do that," the lawyer said. "In the first place I wouldn't want to, thirty-three and a third per cent of it being mine, and in the second place you have no authority."

"I'm the chief of police," Grande said doggedly. "I don't want to spill any blood—"

"Don't flash your badge at me, Vince," Lynch said. Negus had finished counting the money and the lawyer took one of the piles and put it in various pockets. "I said you had no authority. Bank robbery is a federal offense. Not that I admit there's been a robbery. But if you suspect a crime it's your duty to go to the proper authorities. The FBI would be indicated, if you know where they can be reached."

"Yeah," Joe Negus said. "Go take a flying jump for yourself, Chief."

"Listen, you cheap crook—"

"Hardly cheap, Vince," Lynch said. "And not even a crook, in my professional opinion. Mr. Negus pleads extra-territoriality."

That was the start of Superior's crime wave.

Somebody broke the plate-glass window of George Tocher's dry-goods store and got away with blankets, half a dozen overcoats and several sets of woolen underwear.

A fuel-oil truck disappeared from the street outside of Dabney Brothers' and was found abandoned in the morning. About nine hundred gallons had been drained out—as if someone had filled his cellar tank and a couple of his neighbors'.

The back door of the supermarket was forced and somebody made off with a variety of groceries. The missing goods would have just about filled one car.

Each of these crimes was understandable—Superior's growing food and fuel shortage and icy temperatures had led a few people to desperation.

But there were other incidents. Somebody smashed the window at Kimbrough's Jewelry Store and snatched a display of medium-priced watches.

Half a dozen young vandals sneaked into the Catholic Church and began toppling statues of the saints. When they were surprised by Father Brian they fled, bombarding him with prayer books. One of the books shattered a stained-glass window depicting Christ dispensing loaves and fishes.

Somebody started a fire in the movie-house balcony and nearly caused a panic.

Vincent Grande rushed from place to place, investigating, but rarely learned enough to make an arrest. The situation was becoming unpleasant. Superior had always been a friendly place to live, where everyone knew everyone else, at least to say hello to, but now there was suspicion and fear, not to mention increasing cold and threatened famine.

Everyone was cheered up, therefore, when Mayor Hector Civek announced a mass meeting in Town Square. Bonfires were lit and the reviewing stand that was used for the annual Founders' Day parade was hauled out as a speaker's platform.

Civek was late. The crowd, bundled up against the cold, was stamping their feet and beginning to shout a bit when he arrived. There was a medium-sized cheer as the mayor climbed to the platform.

"Fellow citizens," he began, then stopped to search through his overcoat pockets.

"Well," he went on, "I guess I put the speech in an inside pocket and it's too cold to look for it. I know what it says, anyway."

This brought a few laughs. Don Cort stood near the edge of the crowd and watched the people around him. They mostly had a no-nonsense look about them, as if they were not going to be satisfied with more oratory.

Civek said, "I'm not going to keep you standing in the cold and tell you what you already know—how our food supplies are dwindling, how we're using up our stocks of coal and fuel oil with no immediate hope of replacement—you know all that."

"We sure do, Hector," somebody called out.

"Yes; so, as I say, I'm not going to talk about what the problem is. We don't need words—we need action."

He paused as if he expected a cheer, or applause, but the crowd merely waited for him to go on.

"If Superior had been hit by a flood or a tornado," Civek said, "we could look to the Red Cross and the State or Federal Government for help. But we've been the victims of a far greater misfortune, torn from the bosom of Mother Earth and flung—"

"Oh, come on, Hector," an old woman said. "We're getting froze."

"I'm sorry about that, Mrs. Potts," Civek said. "You should be home where it's warm."

"We ran out of coal for the furnace and now we're running out of logs. Are you going to do something about that?"

"I'll tell you what I'm going to do, Mrs. Potts, for you and all the other wonderful people here tonight. We're going to put a stop to this lawlessness we never had before. We're going to make Superior a place to be proud of. Superior has changed—risen, you might say, to a new status. We're more than a town, now. We're free and separate, not only from Ohio, but from the United States.

"We're a sovereign place, a—a sovereignty, and we need new methods to cope with new conditions, to restore law and order, to see that all our subjects—our citizen-subjects—are provided for."

The crowd had become hushed as Civek neared his point.

"To that noble end," Civek went on, "I dedicate myself, and I take this momentous step and hereby proclaim the existence of the Kingdom of Superior..." He paused to take a deep breath. "...and proclaim myself its first King."

He stopped. His oratory had carried him to a climax and he didn't quite know where to go from there. Maybe he expected cheers to carry him over, but none came. There was complete silence except for the crackling of the bonfires.

But after a moment there was a shuffling of feet and a whispering that grew to a murmur. Then out of the murmur came derisive shouts and catcalls.

"King Hector the First!" somebody hooted. "Long live the king!"

The words could have been gratifying but the tone of voice was all wrong.

"Where's Hector's crown?" somebody else cried. "Hey, Jack, did you forget to bring the crown?"

"Yeah," Jack said. "I forgot. But I got a rope over on my truck. We could elevate him that way."

Jack was obviously joking, but a group of men in another part of the crowd pushed toward the platform. "Yeah," one of them said, "let's string him up."

A woman at the back of the crowd screamed. Two hairy figures about five feet tall appeared from the darkness. They were kangaroo-like, with long tails. No one tried to stop them, and the creatures reached the platform and pulled Hector down. They placed him between them and, their way clear now, began to hop away.

Their hops grew longer as they reached the edge of the square. Their leaps had become prodigious as they disappeared in the direction of North Lake, Civek in his heavy coat looking almost like one of them.

Don Cort couldn't tell whether the creatures were kidnaping Civek or rescuing him.

CHAPTER EIGHT

Hector Civek hadn't been found by the time Judge Helms' court convened at 10:00 A.M.

Joe Negus was there, wearing a new suit and looking confident. His confederate, Hank Stacy, was obviously trying to achieve the same poise but not succeeding. Jerry Lynch, their lawyer, was talking to Ed Clark.

Don Cort took a seat the editor had saved for him in the front row. Alis Garet came in and sat next to him. "I cut my sociology class," she told him. "Anybody find His Majesty yet?"

"No," Don said. "Who gave him that crackpot idea?"

"He's had big ideas ever since he ran for the State Assembly. He got licked then, but this is the first time he's been kidnaped. Or should it be kanganaped? Poor Hector. I shouldn't joke about it."

Judge Helms, who was really a justice of the peace, came in through a side door and the clerk banged his gavel. But the business of the court did not get under way immediately. Someone burst in from the street and shouted:

"He's back! Civek's back!"

The people at the rear of the room rushed out to see. In a moment they were crowding back in behind Hector Civek's grand entrance.

"Oh, no," Alis said. "Don't tell me he made it this time!"

Civek was wearing the trappings of royalty. He walked with dignity down the aisle, an ermine robe on his shoulders, a crown on his head and a scepter in his right hand.

He nodded benignly about him. "Good morning, Judge," he said. To the clerk he said, "Frank, see to our horses, will you?"

"Horses?" the clerk said, blinking.

"Our royal coach is without, and the horses need attending to," Civek said patiently. "You don't think a king walks, do you?"

The clerk went out, puzzled. Judge Helms took off his pince-nez and regarded the spectacle of Hector Civek in ermine.

"What is all this, Hector?" he asked. "You weren't serious about that king business, were you? Nice to see you back safe, by the way."

"We would prefer to be addressed the first time as Your Majesty, Judge," Civek said. "After that you can call us sir."

"Us?" the judge asked. "Somebody with you?"

"The royal 'we,'" Civek said. "I see I'll have to issue a proclamation on the proper forms of address. I mean, *we'll* have to. Takes a bit of getting used to, doesn't it?"

"Quite a bit," the judge agreed. "But right now, if you don't mind, this court is in session and has a case before it. Suppose you make your royal self comfortable and we'll get on with it—as soon as my clerk is back from attending to the royal horses."

The clerk returned and whispered in the judge's ear. Helms looked at Civek and shook his head. "Six of them, eh? I'll have a look later. Right now we've got a bank robbery case on the calendar."

Vincent Grande talked and Jerry Lynch talked and Judge Helms listened and looked up statutes and pursed his lips thoughtfully. Joe Negus cleaned his nails. Hank Stacy bit his.

Finally the judge said, "I hate to admit this, but I'm afraid I must agree with you, counselor. The alleged crime contravened no local statute, and in the absence of a representative of the Federal Government I must regretfully dismiss the charges."

Joe Negus promptly got up and began to walk out.

"Just a minute there, varlet!"

It was Hector Civek doing his king bit.

Negus, who probably had been called everything else in his life, paused and looked over his shoulder.

"Approach!" Civek thundered.

"Nuts, Your Kingship," Negus said. "Nobody stops me now." But before he got to the door something stopped him in mid-stride.

Civek had pointed his scepter at Negus in that instant. Negus, stiff as a stop-action photograph, toppled to the floor.

"Now," Civek said, motioning to Judge Helms to vacate the bench, "we'll dispense some royal justice."

He sat down, arranging his robes and shifting his heavy crown. "Mr. Counselor Lynch, we take it you represent the defendants?"

"Yes, Your Majesty," said the lawyer, an adaptable man. "What happened to Negus, sir? Is he dead?"

"He could have been, if we'd given him another notch. No, he's just suspended. Let him be an example to anyone else who might incur our royal wrath. Now, counselor, we are familiar enough with the case to render an impartial verdict. We find the defendants guilty of bank robbery."

"But Your Majesty," Lynch said, "bank robbery is not a crime under the laws of Superior. I submit that there has been no crime—inasmuch as the incident occurred after Superior became detached from Earth, and therefore from its laws."

"There is the King's Law," Civek said. "We decree bank robbery a crime, together with all other offenses against the county, state and country which are not specifically covered in Superior's statutes."

"Retroactively?" Lynch asked.

"Of course. We will now pronounce sentence. First, restitution of the money, except for ten per cent to the King's Bench. Second, indefinite paralysis for Negus. We'll straighten out his arms and legs so he'll take up less room. Third, probation for Hank Stacy here, with a warning to him to stay out of bad company. Court's adjourned."

Civek wouldn't say where he'd got the costume or the coach-and-six or the paralyzing scepter. He refused to say where the two kangaroo-like creatures had taken him. He allowed his ermine to be fingered, holding the scepter out of reach, talked vaguely about better times to come now that Superior was a monarchy, then ordered his coach.

By royal decree Hank Stacy, who had been inching toward the door, became royal coachman, commanded to serve out his probation in the king's custody. Stacy drove Civek home. No one seemed to remember who had been at the reins when the coach first appeared.

CHAPTER NINE

Ed Clark was setting type for an extra when Don and Alis visited his shop.

King's in Business, the headline said.

"You don't sound like a loyal subject," Don said.

"Can't say I am," Clark admitted. "Guess I won't get to be a royal printer."

"What's the story about?" Alis asked. "The splendid triumph of justice in court this morning?"

"No. Everybody knows all about that already. I've got the inside story—what happens next. Just like *The New York Times*."

"Where'd you get it?" Don asked.

Clark winked. "Like Scotty Reston, I am not at liberty to divulge my sources. Let's just say it was learned authoritatively."

"Well," Alis said, "what does happen next?"

"'His Unconstitutional Majesty, King Hector I, will attempt to prop up his shaky monarchy by seeking an ambassador from the United States, the *Sentry* learned today. Such recognition, if obtained, would be followed immediately by a demand for "foreign aid."

"'It is the thesis of the self-proclaimed king—known until 24 hours ago as just plain Hector—that the satellite status of Superior, the traveling townoid, makes it a potentially effective arm of U. S. diplomacy. King Hector will point out to the State Department the benefits of bolstering Superior's economy, especially during its expected foray over Europe and, barring such misfortune as being shot down en route, into the Soviet domain.

"'The King will not suggest in so many words that Superior would make a good spy platform, but the implication is there. It will also be implied that unless economic aid—which in plain English means food and fuel to keep Superior from starving and freezing to death—is forthcoming from the United States, Superior may choose the path of neutrality...'

"That's as far as I've got," Clark said.

"I suppose the 'path of neutrality' means Superior might consider hiring itself out to the highest bidder?" Don asked.

"That would be one way of putting it," Clark said. "Undiplomatic but accurate."

"How does Civek intend to get his message to Washington?" asked Don, aware that it had already been transmitted to the Pentagon via the transceiver under his collar. "Bottle over the side?"

"My sources tell me they've got WCAV working on short wave. That right, Alis?"

"Don't ask me. I only live there."

"Do you still think Civek is fronting for the Cavalier crowd?" Don asked her.

"I don't remember saying that," she said. "I think I agreed with you when you said Civek was ineffectual. Who do *you* think is behind him? Do you think he's king of the kangaroos?"

"Well," Don said, "they're the ones who took him away last night. And when he came back this morning he had all the trappings. He didn't get that coach-and-six from foreign aid."

Ed Clark said, "This is all very fascinating, kids, but it's not helping me get out my extra. Don, why don't you take the little lady out to lunch? You can continue your theorizing over the blueplate special at the Riverside Inn. Only place in town still open, they tell me."

Doc Bendy was hurrying out of the Riverside Inn as they reached it. He waved to them. "Save your money. His Gracious Majesty is throwing a free lunch for everybody."

"Where?"

"At the palace, of course."

"What palace?" Alis asked.

"The bubble gum factory. He's taken it over."

"Why the gum factory?"

"Cheeky McFerson offered it to him. Not the factory itself but the big old house near the west wing. The mansion that's been closed up since the old man died. They say Cheeky's been given a title as part of the bargain."

"Sir Cheeky?" Alis asked, giggling.

"Something like that. Lord Chicle, maybe, or Baron de Mouthful. Come on. It should be quite a show."

Dozens of people were in the streets, all heading in the same direction. Word of the king's largess spread fast and, on the factory grounds, guards were directing the crowd to a line that disappeared into a side door of the old McFerson mansion.

A flag flew from the top of a pole at the front of the house. It was whipping in a stiff breeze and Don couldn't make out the device, except that a crown formed part of it.

One of the guards recognized Alis Garet and directed her to the front door. She took Doc Bendy and Don by their arms. "Come on," she said. "We're VIP's. Father must have sworn allegiance."

The chief of police was sitting behind a desk in the wide front hall but he now wore a military tunic with a chestful of decorations (including the Good Conduct Medal, Sergeant

Cort noticed), and the visor of his military cap was overrun with gold curlicues.

"Well, Vince," Bendy said. "I see you got in on the ground floor."

"General Sir Vincent Grande, Minister of Defense," Grande said with a stiff little bow, "at your service."

"Enchanted," Bendy said, bowing back. "Tell me, Vince, how do you keep a straight face?"

"I'll overlook that, Bendy, and I'll give you a friendly tip. The country is on a sound basis now and we intend to keep it that way. Obstructionists will be dealt with."

"The country, eh? Well, let's go in and see how it's being run."

A clattery hubbub came from the big room on the right. To Don it sounded like any GI mess hall. It also looked like one. The line of people coming in through the side door helped themselves to tin trays and silverware, then moved slowly past a row of huge pots from which white-coated men and women ladled out food. At the end of the serving line stood Cheeky McFerson, splendid in purple velvet. He was putting a piece of bubble gum on each tray.

On the other side of the room, opposite the servers, King Hector sat on a raised chair, crown on head, scepter in hand, nodding benevolently to anyone who looked at him. On each side of the king, sitting in lower chairs, were members of what must have been his court. Professor Osbert Garet was one of them, and Maynard Rubach, president of the Cavalier Institute of Applied Sciences, was another.

"Oh, dear, there's Father," Alis said in dismay. "What is that silly hat he's wearing? It makes him look like Merlin."

"But Civek doesn't look a bit like King Arthur," Bendy said. "Let's go pay our respects. Straight faces, now."

"Ah, my dear," the king said when he saw Alis. "And gentlemen. Welcome to our court. May we introduce two of our associates? Sir Osbert Garet, Royal Astronaut, and Lord Rubach, Minister of Education."

"Father!" Alis spoke sharply to the Royal Astronaut. "How silly can you get?"

"Now, now, child," the king said reprovingly. "You must not risk our displeasure. For the time being our rule must be absolute—until the safety of our kingdom has been assured. Sir Osbert," he said, "we trust that at a more propitious time you will have a serious talk with your charming but impetuous daughter."

"My liege, I shall deal with her," the Royal Astronaut said, glowering at Alis. "As Your Majesty has so wisely observed, she is but a slip of a girl."

Her father's apparent sincerity left Alis speechless. She looked from Bendy to Don, but they seemed to consider discretion and masklike faces the better part of candor.

"Well spoken, Sir Osbert," the king said. He clapped his hands and a servant jumped. "Dinner for these three. Find a table, my friends, and you will be served."

Don firmly guided Alis away. She had seemed about to explode. They found an empty table out of earshot of the king, and three footmen looking like refugees from *Alice in Wonderland* immediately began to serve them.

Bendy spread a napkin over his lap. "Let's curb our snickers and fill our stomachs," he said, "and later we can go out behind the barn and laugh our heads off. Meanwhile, keep your eyes open."

They were eating meat loaf and potatoes. The meat loaf was so highly spiced that it could have been almost anything.

"I wonder where His Worship got all the grub," Alis said.

"I don't know," Don said, "but it certainly doesn't look as if he needs any foreign aid."

Alis put down her fork suddenly and her eyes got big. She said, "You don't suppose—"

"Suppose what?" Bendy said, spearing a small potato.

"I just had a horrible thought." She laughed feebly. "It's ridiculous, of course, but I wondered if by any chance we were eating Joe Negus."

"Don't be silly," Don said, but he put down his fork too.

"Of course it's ridiculous," Bendy said. "Hector only put Negus to sleep. He didn't kill him. Besides, Joe Negus wouldn't stretch far enough to feed this crowd."

"Is that why you're not eating any more?" Alis asked him.

"Why, no," Bendy said. "It's merely that I've had enough. It's true that Hector could have used his scepter on other transgressors, but—no, I refuse to admit that he's turned cannibal."

"*He* isn't eating," Don pointed out.

"I'll guarantee you he has, though. I've never known Hector to miss a meal. No. Hector may be a fool and a dupe, and power-hungry to boot, but he's not a cruel man, or a deranged one."

"No?" Alis said. "I dare you to ask him what's in the meat loaf."

"All right." Bendy got up. "I'll ask to see the kitchen—to compliment the chef. Want to come?"

"No, thanks. I might be mean to Father again."

She and Don watched Doc Bendy go to the improvised throne and talk to Civek. The king laughed and stood up and he and Bendy crossed the room. They went through a door behind the line of servers.

Don pushed his plate away. "You've certainly spoiled my appetite."

"I'm sorry," Alis said. "Maybe it's hereditary. Look at Father in that idiot hat. Sir Osbert! Honestly, Don, if we ever get back to Earth I'm going to get out of Superior as fast as I can. What's it like in Washington?"

"Dull," he said. "Humid in the summer. And when you've exhausted the national monuments there's nothing to do."

"Nothing? Don't tell me you don't have a girl friend back there. No, *don't* tell me—I don't want to know. Oh, Don, what a terribly boring place this must be for you."

"Boring!" he said. "I've never had such a wild, crazy time in my life. Furthermore," he said, "there's nobody like you back in Washington."

She beamed. "I'd kiss you right here, only Doc Bendy's coming back. Heck, I'll kiss you anyway."

She did.

"Ahem," said Bendy. "Also cough-cough. If you two can spare the time, there's someone I'd like you to meet."

"We're through, for now," Alis said. "Who?"

"One of our hosts. The power behind the shaky throne of Hector the First. I think you'll like him. He has a magnificent tail."

"Hector was very co-operative," Doc Bendy said. "I guess he figured he couldn't keep it a secret for long anyhow, so he decided to be frank. After all, half the town saw them take him away."

"You mean Civek admits he's only a figurehead?" Don asked.

"Oh, he wouldn't admit that. His story is that it's a working arrangement—a treaty of sorts. He's absolute monarch as far as the human inhabitants are concerned, but the kangaroos control Superior as a piece of geography."

"I knew Father couldn't have done it," Alis murmured.

They went down a flight of stairs off the main hall to a basement room. It was luxuriously furnished, as every room in the mansion must have been. There was a rug over inlaid linoleum and a blazing fireplace. A huge round mahogany table stood in the center of the room.

Hector Civek sat in one of the half-dozen leather armchairs drawn up to the table. In another sat a furry, genial-looking blue-gray kangaroo.

Only it wasn't really a kangaroo, Don realized. It was more human than animal in several ways. Its bearing, for instance, had dignity, and its round eyes had intelligence. A thick tail at least three feet long stuck through a space under the backrest of the armchair. As Doc Bendy had said, the tail was magnificent.

Civek nodded and smiled, apparently willing to forget his flare-up at Alis. "I'll introduce you," Civek said. "I mean *we'll* introduce you. Oh, the hell with the royal 'we,' as long I'm among friends. This is Gizl, and what I'm trying to say is that he doesn't speak English. Doesn't talk at all, as far as I can tell. But he understands the language and he can read and write it. That's why all this."

He indicated the letter and number squares on the table. They were from sets of games—Scrabble, Anagrams, I-Qubes, Lotto and poker dice.

"My granddaughter met Gizl, you'll recall," Doc Bendy said. "Either this one or one like him. We don't know yet whether Gizl is a personal name or a generic one."

"Let's find out," Don said. He sat down at the table and began to form squares into a question.

"Wait a minute." Doc Bendy broke up Don's sequence. "The amenities first. Spell out 'Greetings,' or some such things. Manners, boy."

"Sorry." Don started over. He spelled Greetings, then Alis Garet, then Don Cort, and pointed from the squares to Alis and himself. "I assume you've already introduced yourself?" he asked Bendy.

Bendy nodded and the kangaroo-like creature inclined his furry head in acknowledgment to Alis and Don. Then he—

Don had already stopped thinking of the creature as an "it"—formed two words with his tapering, black-nailed fingers.

Pleasant, he communicated. "Gizl." And he tapped his chest.

Don turned to Bendy. "Now can I ask him?"

"With His Majesty's permission," Bendy said solemnly.

Hector nodded. Don left the three names intact, distributing the rest, then put three squares together to spell *Man*. He pointed to the word and then to Civek, Bendy, Alis and himself, excluding the creature.

"Well, I like that!" Alis said. "Do I look like a man?"

"Let's keep it simple, woman," Don said.

The creature nodded and pointed again to Gizl, then to himself, "He doesn't understand," Don said.

"It's quite possible his people don't have individual names," Bendy said. "Let's call him Gizl for now and go on."

"Okay." Don thought for a moment, then formed a question. "Might as well get basic," he said.

Q. Are you from earth.

A. No.

At the risk of irritating the others, Don repeated the questions and answers aloud for the benefit of his eavesdropper in the Pentagon.

Q. Are you from solar system

A. Not yours

Q. When did you reach earth

A. 1948 your calendar

Q. Why

A. Friendship

Q. Why has no one seen you sooner

A. Fear

Q. You mean you frightened our people

A. No I mean fear of your people

Q. Why

A. Gizl resemble earth animals

Q. Was superior the first place you landed

A. No

Q. Where was it

A. Australia

"The home of the kangaroo," Doc Bendy said. "No wonder they had a bad time. I can imagine some stockman in the outback taking umbrage at a kangaroo asserting its equality. Let me talk to him a while, Don."

Q. How many are there of you

A. Many

Q. How many

A. No specific comment

Q. Are you responsible for raising superior

A. Entirely

Q. How

A. Impossible to explain with these

Q. Where is superior going

A. East for now

Q. And later

A. No specific comment

Q. 3000 lives are in your hands

A. Gizls have no malevolent designs

Q. Thanks. You said friendship brought you. What else.

A. Trade. Cultural exchange

Q. What have you to trade

A. Will discuss this later with duly constituted authority

Q. Who. King Hector

A. Terminating interview with good will assurances

"Wait," Alis said. "I haven't had a chance to talk to him." She formed letters into words. "I don't think he's being very frank with us but I have a few random questions."

Q. How many sexes have Gizls

A. Three

Q. Male female and

A. Neuter

Q. Are there babies among you

A. Babies are neuter and develop according to need

Q. Confidentially what do you think of fathers science

A. Unfathomable our meager knowledge

Q. Flatterer

A. Ending conversation with pleasant regard

Q. Likewise

Gizl slid back his chair and got up. King Hector stood and bowed as Gizl, who had nodded politely to each in turn, walked manlike, without hopping, to a corner of the room which then sank out of sight.

"He's quite a guy, that Gizl," Hector said, taking off his crown and putting it on the table. "Makes me sweat," he said, wiping his forehead.

"Are you the duly constituted authority?" Bendy asked him.

"Who else? Somebody's got to be in charge till we get Superior back to Earth."

"Sure," Bendy said, "but you don't have to rig yourself up in ermine. I also have a sneaking suspicion that you aren't exactly anxious to get Superior down in a hurry."

"I'll overlook that remark for old time's sake. But I defend the kingship. A show of force was necessary to prevent crime from running rampant."

"Maybe," Bendy said. "Anyhow I appreciate your frankness in introducing us to Gizl and what he modestly describes as his meager knowledge. Since you've already admitted that he's the one who provided the big feed, will you ease Alis's mind now and assure her that what she was eating wasn't Negusburger?"

"Negusburger?" The king laughed. "Is that what you thought, Alis?"

"Not really," she said. "But I couldn't help wondering where all the food came from all of a sudden."

"Over here." The king led them to the corner where Gizl had sunk from sight. The top of the elevator, now level with the floor, blended exactly with the linoleum tile. "I don't know how it works, but Gizl and his people have their headquarters down there somewhere. All I have to do is place the order and up comes food or whatever I need. Would you like to try it?"

"Love to," Bendy said. "What shall I ask for?"

"Anything."

"Anything?"

"Anything at all."

"Well." Bendy looked impressed. "This will take a moment of thought. How about a gallon—no, as long as I'm asking I might as well ask for a keg—of rum, 151 proof."

Up it came, complete with spigot and tankard.

"Fabulous!" Bendy said. He rolled it out of the elevator and the elevator went down again.

"Let me try!" Alis said. "If Doc can get a keg, I ought to be able to have—oh, say a pint of Channel No. 5. Would that be too extravagant?"

"A simple variation in formula, I should think," the king said.

What came up for Alis didn't look in the least like an expensive Paris perfume. In fact, it looked like a lard pail with a quantity of liquid sloshing lazily in it. But its aroma belied its looks.

"Oh, heaven!" Alis said. "Smell it!" She lifted it by its handle, stuck a finger in it and rubbed behind each ear.

"It's a bit overpowering by the pint," Bendy said. He'd drained off part of a tankard of rum and looked quite at peace with the world. "You'd better get yourself a chaperone, Alis, if you're going to carry that around with you."

"I'll admit they're not very good in the packaging department, but that's just a quibble. Could I have—how many ounces in a pint?—sixteen one-ounce stoppered bottles? And a little funnel?"

"Easiest thing in the world," the king said. "Don? Anything you'd like at the same time? Save it a trip."

"I've got an idea, Your Majesty, but I don't know whether you'd approve. Even though I work in a bank, I've never seen a ten thousand dollar bill. Do you think they could whip one up?"

"I really don't know," Hector said. "It could upset the economy if we let the money get out of hand. But we can always send it right back. Let's see what happens."

The elevator came up with the bottles, the funnel and a green and gold bill.

It was, on the face of it, a ten thousand dollar bill. But the portrait was that of Hector Civek, crowned and ermined. And the legend on it was:

"Payable to Bearer on Demand, Ten Thousand Dollars. This Note is Legal Tender for all Debts, Public and Private, and is Redeemable in Lawful Money at the Treasury of the Kingdom of Superior. (Signed) Gizl, Secretary of the Treasury."

CHAPTER TEN

D on didn't know what he might learn by skulking around the freezing grounds of Hector's palace in the faint moonlight. He hoped for a glimpse of the kangaroo-Gizl to see if he were as sincere off-guard as he had been during their interview.

But his peering into basement windows had revealed nothing, and he was about to head back to the campus for a night's sleep when someone called his name.

It was a girl's voice, from above. He looked up. Red-headed Geneva Jervis was leaning out of one of the second-story windows.

"Well, hello," he said. "What are you doing up there?"

"I've sworn fealty," she said. "Come on up."

"What?" he said. "How?"

She disappeared from his sight, then reappeared. "Here." She dropped a rope ladder.

Don climbed it, feeling Like Romeo. "Where'd you get this?"

"They've got them in all the rooms. Fire escapes. Old McFerson was a precautious man, evidently." She pulled the rope back in.

Jen Jervis had a spacious bedroom. She wore a dressing gown.

"What do you mean, you swore fealty?" Don asked. "To Hector?"

"Sure. What better way to find out what he's up to? Besides, I was getting fed up with that dormitory at Cavalier.

No privacy. House mothers creeping around all the time. Want a drink?"

Don saw that she had a half-full glass on the dresser. Next to the glass stood a bottle of bourbon with quite a bit gone from it.

"Why not?" he said. "Let's drink and be merry, for tomorrow we may freeze to death."

"Or be shot down by Reds." She poured him a stiff one. "Here's to happy endings."

He sipped his drink and she swallowed half of hers.

"I didn't picture you as the drinking type, Jen."

"Revise the picture. Come sit down." She backed to the big double bed and relaxed into it, lying on one elbow.

Don sat next to her, but upright. "Tell me about this fealty deal. What did you have to do?"

"Oh, renounce my American citizenship and swear to protect Superior against all enemies, foreign and domestic. The usual thing."

"Have you got a title yet? Are you Dame Jervis?"

"Not yet." She smiled. "I think I'm on probation. They know I'm close to Bobby and they'd like to have him on their side, for all their avowed independence. They're not so terribly convinced that Superior's going to stay up forever. They're hedging their bets, it looks to me."

"It looks to me that maybe Bobby Thebold might not understand. He's the kind of man who demands absolute fealty, from what I've seen of him."

"Oh, to hell with Bobby Thebold." Jen took another swallow. "He's not here. He's had plenty of time to come, if he was going to, and he hasn't. To hell with him. Let me get you another drink."

"No, thanks. This will do me fine." He drank it and set the empty glass on the floor. Jen drank off the last of hers and put her glass next to his.

"Relax," she said. "I'm not going to bite you." She lay back and her dressing gown opened in a V as far as the belt. She obviously wasn't wearing anything under the gown.

Don looked away self-consciously.

Jen laughed. "What's the matter, boy? No red blood?" She rolled herself off the end of the bed and went to the dresser. "Another drink?"

"Don't you think you've had enough?"

She shook her red hair violently. "Drinking is as drinking does. Trouble is, nobody's doing anything."

"Exactly. Everybody's acting as if Superior's one big pleasure dome. Civek's on the throne and all's well with his little world. Even you've joined the parade. Why? I don't buy that double-agent explanation."

She was looking in the bureau mirror at the reflection of the top of her head, peering up from under her eyebrows. "I'm going to have to touch up the tresses pretty soon or I won't be a redhead any more." She looked at his reflection. "You don't like me, do you, Donny-boy?"

"I never said that."

"You don't have to say it. But I don't blame you. I don't like myself sometimes. I'm a cold fish. A cold, dedicated fish. Or I was. I've decided to change my ways."

"I can see that."

"Can you?" She turned around and leaned against the bureau, holding her glass. "How do you see me now?"

"As an attractive woman with a glass in her hand. I wonder which is doing the talking."

"Rhetorical questions at this time of night, Donny? I think it's me talking, not the whisky. We'll know better in the sober light of morning, won't we?"

"If that's an invitation," Don began, "I'm afraid—"

Her eyes blazed at him. "I think you're the rudest man I ever met. *And* the most boorish." She tossed off the rest of her drink, then began to cry.

"Now, Jen—" He went to her and patted her shoulder awkwardly.

"Oh, Don." She put her head against his chest and wept. His arms automatically went around her, comfortingly.

Then he realized that Jen's muffled sobs were going direct to the Pentagon through his transceiver. That piece of electronics equipment taped to his skin, he told himself, was the least of the reasons why he could not have accepted Jen's invitation—if it had been an invitation.

He lifted her chin from his chest to spare the man in the Pentagon any further sobs, which must have been reaching him in crescendo. Jen's face was tear-stained. She looked into his eyes for a second, then fastened her mouth firmly on his.

There was nothing a gentleman could do, Don thought, except return the kiss. Rude, was he?

Jen broke away first. "What's that?" she said.

Don opened his eyes and his glance went automatically to the door. It would not have surprised him to see King Hector coming through it in his royal night clothes. But Jen was staring out the window. He turned.

The sky was bright as day over in the direction of the golf course. Don made out a pinpoint of brighter light.

"It's a star shell," he said. "A flare."

They went to the window and leaned out, looking past a corner of the bubble gum factory.

"What's it for?" Jen asked.

Don pointed. "There. That's what for."

"A blimp!" she said. "It's landing!"

"Is it an Air Force job? I can't make out the markings."

"I think I can," Jen said. "They're—PP."

"Private Pilots! Senator Bobby the Bold!"

Jen Jervis clutched his arm. "S.O.B.!" she whispered fiercely.

Don Cort was down the rope fire escape and away from the mansion before it woke up to the invasion. As he crossed the railroad spur he had a glimpse of Jen Jervis hauling up the rope and of lights going on elsewhere in the building. There was a lot of whistle-blowing and shouting and a lone shot which didn't seem to be aimed at him.

Don waited at the spur, behind a boxcar, to see how the Hectorites would react to the landing of the blimp, A few men gathered at the front gate and looked nervously into the sky and toward the golf course. Others joined them, armed with shotguns, pistols, and a rifle or two, but not with King Hector's paralysis gadget.

It was clear that Hector had no intention of starting a battle. His men apparently were under orders only to guard the mansion and the bubble gum factory. No one even went to see what the blimp was up to.

Don found as he neared the golf course that the people from the blimp apparently had no immediate plan to attack, either. He found a sand trap to lie down in. From it he could watch without being seen. The star shell had died out but he could see the blimp silhouetted against the sky. Men in battle dress were establishing a perimeter around the clubhouse. Each carried a weapon of some kind. It was all very dim.

Don remembered his communicator. "Cort here," he said softly. "Do you read me?"

"Affirmative," a voice said. Don didn't recognize it. He described the landing and asked, "Is this an authorized landing or is it Senator Thebold's private party?"

"Negative," said the voice from the Pentagon, irritatingly GI.

"Negative *what?*" Don said. "You mean Thebold *is* leading it?"

"Affirmative," said the voice.

"What's he up to?" Don asked.

"Negative," the voice said.

Don blew up. "If you mean you don't know, why the hell don't you say so? Who is this, anyhow?"

"This happens to be Major Johns, the O.O.D., Sergeant, and if you know what's good for you—"

Don stopped listening because a man in battle dress, apparently attracted by his voice, was standing on the green, looking down into the bunker where Don lay, pointing a carbine at him.

"I'll have to hang up now, Major," Don said quietly. "Something negative has just happened to me. I've been captured."

The man with the carbine shouted down to Don, "Okay, come out with your hands over your head."

Don did so. He hoped he was doing it affirmatively enough. He had no wish to be shot by one of the Senator's men, regardless of whether that man was authorized or unauthorized.

Senator Thebold sat at a desk in the manager's office of the Raleigh Country Club. He wore a leather trench coat and a fur hat. Wing commander's insignia glittered on his shoulders and a cartridge belt was buckled around his waist. A holster hung from it but Thebold had the heavy .45 on the desk in front of it. He motioned to Don to sit down. Two guards stood at the door.

"Name?" Thebold snapped.

Don decided to use his own name but pretend to be a local yokel.

"Donald Cort."

"What were you doing out there?"

"I saw the lights."

"Who were you talking to in the sand trap?"

"Nobody. I sometimes talk to myself."

"Oh, you do. Do you ever talk to yourself about a man named Osbert Garet or Hector Civek?" Thebold looked at a big map of Superior that had been pinned to the wall, thus giving Don the benefit of his strong profile.

"Hector's the king now," Don said. "Things got pretty bad before that but we got enough to eat now."

"Where did the food come from?"

Don shrugged.

Thebold drummed his fingers on the desk. "You're not exactly a fount of information, are you? What do you do for a living?"

"I used to work in the gum factory but I got laid off."

"Do you know Geneva Jervis?"

"Who's he?" Don said innocently.

Thebold stood up in obvious irritation. "Take this man to O. & I.," he said to one of the guards. "We've got to make a start some place. Are there any others?"

"Four or five," the guard said.

"Send me the brightest-looking one. Give this one and the rest a meal and a lecture and turn them loose. It doesn't look as if Civek is going to give us any trouble right away and there isn't too much we can do before daylight."

The guard led Don out of the room and pinned a button on his lapel. It said: *Bobby the Bold in Peace and War.*

"What's O. & I.?" Don asked him.

"Orientation and Integration. Nobody's going to hurt you. We're here to end partition, that's all."

"End partition?"

"Like in Ireland. Keep Superior in the USA. They'll tell you all about it at O. & I. Then you tell your friends. Want some more buttons?"

Don was fed, lectured, and released, as promised.

Early the next morning, after a cup of coffee with Alis Garet at Cavalier's cafeteria, he started back for the golf course. Alis, in a class-cutting mood, went with him.

The glimpses of the Thebold Plan which Don had had from O. & I. were being put into practice. Reilly Street, which provided a boundary line between Raleigh Country Club and the gum-factory property, had been transformed into a midway.

The Thebold forces had strung bunting and set up booths along the south side of the street. Hector's men, apparently relieved to find that the battle was to be psychological rather than physical, rushed to prepare rival attractions on their side. A growing crowd thronged the center of Reilly Street. Some wore Thebold buttons. Some wore other buttons, twice as big, with a smiling picture of Hector I on them. Some wore both.

The sun was bright but the air was bitingly cold. As a result one of the most popular booths was on Hector's side of the street where Cheeky McFerson was giving away an apparently inexhaustible supply of hand-warmers. Cheeky urged everybody to take two, one for each pocket, and threw in handfuls of bubble gum.

Two of Hector's men set up ladders and strung a banner across two store-fronts. It said in foot-high letters: Kingdom of Superior, Land of Plenty.

A group of Thebold troubleshooters watched, then rushed away and reappeared with brushes and paint. They transformed an advertising sign to read, in letters two feet high: Superior, U.S.A., Home of the Free.

Hawkers on opposite sides of the midway vied to give away hot dogs, boiled ears of corn, steaming coffee, hot chocolate, candy bars, and popcorn.

"There's a smart one." Alis pointed to a sign in Thebold territory. *The Gripe Room* it said over a vacant store. The Senator's men had set up desks and chairs inside and long lines had already formed.

Apparently a powerful complaint had been among the first to be registered because a Thebold man was galvanized into action. He ran out of the store and within minutes the sign painters were at work again. Their new banner, hoisted to dry in the sun, proclaimed: Blimp Mail.

Underneath, in smaller letters, it said: *How long since you've heard from your loved ones on Earth? The Thebold Blimp will carry your letters and small packages. Direct daily connections with U. S. Mail.*

"You have to admire them," Alis said. "They're really organized."

"One's as bad as the other," Don said. Impartially, he was eating a Hector hot dog and drinking Thebold coffee. "Have you noticed the guns in the upstairs windows?"

"No. You mean on the Senator's side?"

"Both sides. Don't stare."

"I see them now. Do you see any Gizl-sticks? The thing Hector used on Negus?"

"No. Just conventional old rifles and shotguns. Let's hope nobody starts anything."

"Look," Alis said, grabbing Don by the arm. "Isn't that Ed Clark going into the Gripe Room?"

"It sure is. Gathering material for another powerful editorial, I guess."

But within minutes Clark's visit had provoked another bustle of activity. Two of Thebold's men dashed out of the renovated store and off toward the country club. They came back with the Senator himself, making his first public appearance.

Thebold strode down the center of the midway, wearing his soft aviator's helmet with the goggles pushed up on his forehead and his silk scarf fluttering behind him. A group of small boys followed him, imitating his self-confident walk and scrambling occasionally for the Thebold buttons he threw to them. The Senator went into the Gripe Room.

"Looks as if Ed has wangled an interview with the great man himself," Alis said.

"You didn't say anything to Clark about our talk with the Gizl, did you?"

"I did mention it to him," Alis said. "Was that bad?"

"Half an hour ago I would have said no. Now I'm not so sure."

A speaker's platform had been erected on the Senator's side of Reilly Street, and now canned but stirring band music was blaring out of a loudspeaker. Thebold came out of the Gripe Room and mounted the platform. A fair-sized crowd was waiting to hear him.

Thebold raised his arms as if he were stilling a tumult. The music died away and Thebold spoke.

"My good friends and fellow Americans," the Senator began.

Then a Hectorite sound-apparatus started to blare directly across the street. The sound of hammering added to the disruption as workmen began to set up a rival speaker's platform. Then the music on the north side of Reilly Street became a triumphal march and Hector I made his entrance.

Thebold spoke on doggedly. Don heard an occasional phrase through the din. "...reunion with the USA...end this un-American, this literal partition..."

But many in the crowd had turned to watch Hector, who was magnificent and warm-looking in his ermine robe.

"Loyal subjects of Superior, I exhort you not to listen to this outsider who has come to meddle in our affairs," Hector said. "What can he offer that your king has not provided? You have security, inexhaustible food supplies and, above all, independence!"

Thebold increased his volume and boomed:

"Ah, but *do* you have independence, my friends? Ask your puppet king who provides this food—and for what price? And how secure *do* you feel as you whip through the atmosphere like an unguided missile? You're over the Atlantic now. Who knows at what second the controls may break down and dump us all into the freezing water?"

Hector pushed his crown back on his head as if it were a derby hat. "Who asked the Senator here? Let me remind you that he does not even represent our former—and I emphasize *former*—State of Ohio. We all know him as a political adventurer, but never before has he attempted to meddle in the affairs of another country!"

"And you know what lies beyond Western Europe," Thebold said. "Eastern Europe and Russia. Atheistic, communistic Red Russia. Is that where you'd like to come down? For that's where you're heading under Hector Civek's so-called leadership. King Hector, he calls himself. Let me remind you, friends, that if there is anything the Soviet Russians hate more than a democracy, it's a *monarchy*! I don't like to think what your chances would be if you came down in Kremlinland. Remember what they did to the Czars."

Then Senator Bobby Thebold played his ace:

"But there's an even worse possibility, my poor misguided friends. And that's for the creatures behind Hector Civek to decide to go back home—and take off into outer space. Has Hector told you about the creatures? He has not. Has he told you they're aliens from another planet? He has not. Some of you have seen them—these kangaroo-like creatures who, for their own nefarious purposes, made Hector what he is today.

"But, my friends, these are not the cute and harmless kangaroos that abound in the land of our friendly ally, Australia. No. These are intelligent alien beings who have no use for us at all, and who have brazenly stolen a piece of American territory and are now in the process of making off with it."

A murmur came from the crowd and they looked over their shoulders at Hector, whose oratory had run down and who seemed unsure how to answer.

"Yes, my friends," Thebold went on, "you may well wonder what your fate will be in the hands of that power-mad ex-mayor of yours. A few thousand feet more of altitude and Superior will run out of air. Then you'll really be free of the good old U.S.A. because you'll be dead of suffocation. That, my friends—"

At that point somebody took a shot at Senator Bobby Thebold. It missed him, breaking a second-story window behind him.

Immediately a Thebold man behind that window smashed the rest of the glass and fired back across Reilly Street, over the heads of the crowd.

People screamed and ran. Don grabbed Alis and pulled her away from the immediate zone of fire. They looked back from behind a truck which, until a minute ago, had been dispensing hot buttered popcorn.

"Hostilities seem to have commenced," Alis said. She gave a nervous laugh. "I guess it's my fault for blabbing to Ed Clark."

"It was bound to happen, sooner or later," Don said. "I hope nobody gets hurt."

Evidently neither Thebold nor Hector personally had any such intention. Both had clambered down from the platforms and disappeared. Most of the crowd had fled too, heading east toward the center of town, but a few, like Alis and Don, had merely taken cover and were waiting to see what would happen next.

Sporadic firing continued. Then there was a concentration of shooting from the Senator's side, and a dozen or more of Thebold's men made a quick rush across the street and into the stores and buildings on the north side. In a few minutes they returned, under another protective burst, with prisoners.

"Slick," Don said. "Hector's being outmaneuvered."

"I wonder why the Gizls aren't helping him."

The Thebold loudspeaker came to life. "Attention!" it boomed in the Senator's voice. "Anyone who puts down his arms will be given safe conduct to the free side of Reilly Street. Don't throw away your life for a dictator. Come over to the side of Americanism and common sense." There was a pause, and the voice added: "No reprisals."

The firing stopped.

The Thebold loudspeaker began to play *On the Sunny Side of the Street.*

But nobody crossed over. Nor was there any further firing from Hector's side.

Lay Down Your Arms, the loudspeaker blared in another tune from tin-pan alley.

When it became clear that Hector's forces had withdrawn completely from the Reilly Street salient, Thebold's men crossed in strength.

They worked their way block by block to the grounds of the bubble gum factory and proceeded to lay siege to it.

With Hector Civek immobilized, Senator Bobby Thebold went looking for Geneva Jervis, accompanied by two armed guards.

He was trailed by the usual pack of small boys, several of them dressed in imitation of their hero, in helmets, silk-like scarves and toy guns at hips.

Alis, unable to reach the besieged palace to see if her father was safe, had asked Don to go back with her to Cavalier after the Battle of Reilly Street. Her mother told Alis that the professor was not only safe on the campus but had resigned his post as Royal Astronaut at Hector's court.

"Father broke with Hector?" Alis asked. "Good for him! But why?"

"He and Dr. Rubach just up and walked out," Mrs. Caret said. "That's all I know. Your father never explains these things to me. But if my intuition means anything, the professor is up to one of his tricks again. He's been locked up in his lab all day."

The campus had an air of expectancy about it. Students and instructors went from building to building, exchanging knowing looks or whispered conversations.

A rally was in progress in front of the Administration Building when Senator Thebold arrived. Don and Alis joined the group of listeners for camouflage and pretended to pay attention to what the speaker, an intense young man on the back of a pickup truck, was saying.

"The time has come," he said, "for men and women of, uh, perspicacity to shun the extremes and tread the middle path. To avoid excesses as represented on the one hand by the, uh, paternalistic dictatorship of the Hectorites, and on the other by the, uh, pseudo-democracy of Senator Thebold which resorts to force when thwarted. I proclaim, therefore, the course of reason, the way of science and truth as exemplified by the, uh, the Garet-Rubach, uh—"

Senator Thebold had been listening at the edge of the little crowd. He spoke up.

"The Garet-Rubach Axis?" he suggested.

The speaker gave him a cold stare. "And who are you?"

"Senator Robert Thebold, representing pseudo-democracy, as you call it. Speak on, my young friend. Like Voltaire, I will defend to the death—but you know what Voltaire said."

"Yes, sir," the speaker said, abashed. "No offense intended, Senator."

"Of course you intended offense," Thebold said. "Stick to your guns, man. Free academic discussion must never be curtailed. But at the moment I'm more interested in meeting your Professor Garet. Where is he?"

"In—in the bell tower, sir. Right over there." He pointed. "But you can't go in. No one can." He looked at Alis as if for confirmation. She shook her head.

"We'll see about that," the Senator said. "Carry on with your free and open discussion. And remember, stick to your guns. Sorry I can't stay."

He headed for the bell tower, followed by his guards.

Alis waited till he had gone in, then tugged at Don's sleeve. "Come on. Let's see the fun."

"Alis," the speaker called to her, "was that really Senator Thebold?"

"Sure was. But what's this Garet-Rubach Axis? What's everybody up to?"

"Not Axis. That was Thebold's propaganda word. It's a movement of—oh, never mind. You don't appreciate your own father."

"You can say that again. Come on, Don."

As Alis closed the door to the bell tower behind them, they heard Professor Garet's voice from above.

"Attention interlopers," it said. "You have come unasked and now you find yourself paralyzed, unable to move a muscle except to breathe."

"Stay down here," Alis whispered. "There's a sort of vestibule one flight up. That's where Thebold must have got it. Father spends all his spare time guarding his holy of holies. Nobody gets past the vestibule." She frowned. "But I didn't know he had a paralysis thing, too."

"He probably swiped it from Hector before he broke with him," Don said.

Professor Garet's voice came again. "I shall now pass among you and relieve you of your weapons. Why, if it isn't Senator Thebold and his strong-arm crew! I'm honored, Senator. Here we are: three archaic .45's disposed of. Very soon now you'll have the pleasure of seeing a scientific weapon in action."

Don, standing with Alis on the steps of the Administration Building, didn't know whether to be impressed or amused by the giant machine Professor Garet had assembled. It was mounted on the flat bed of an old Reo truck, and various parts of it went skyward in a dozen directions. Garet had driven it onto the campus from a big shed behind the bell tower.

The machine's crowning glory was a big bowl-shaped sort of thing that didn't quite succeed in looking like a radar scanner. It was at the end of a universal joint which permitted it to aim in any direction.

"What's it supposed to do?" Don asked.

"From what I gather," Alis said, "it's Hector's paralysis thing, adapted for distance. Only of course nobody admits Father stole it. It's supposed to have antigravity powers, too, like whatever it was that took Superior up in the first place. Naturally I don't believe a word of it."

"But where's he going with it?"

"He's ready to take on all comers, I gather. Please don't try to make sense out of it. It's only Father."

The young man who had addressed the student rally took over the driver's seat and Professor Garet hoisted himself into a bucket seat at the rear of the truck near a panel which presumably operated the machine. Maynard Rubach sat next to the driver. The small army of dedicated students who had been assembling fell in behind the truck. They were unarmed, except with faith.

Senator Thebold and his two former bodyguards, de-paralyzed, sat trussed up in the back of a weapons carrier, looking disgusted with everything.

"Are we ready?" Professor Garet called.

A cheer went up.

"Then on to the enemy—in the name of science!"

Don shook his head. "But even if this crazy machine could knock out Hector's and Thebold's men and the Garet-Rubach Axis reigns supreme, then what? Does he claim he can get Superior back to Earth?"

Alis said only, "Please, Don..."

The forces of science were ready to roll. There had been an embarrassing moment when the old Reo's engine died, but a student worked a crank with a will and it roared back to life.

The Garet machine, the weapons carrier and the foot soldiers moved off the campus and onto Shaws Road toward Broadway and the turn-off for the country club.

They met an advance party of the Thebold forces just north of McEntee Street. There were about twenty of them, armed with carbines and submachine guns. As soon as they spotted the weird armada from Cavalier they dropped to the ground, weapons aimed.

Senator Thebold rose in his seat. "Hold your fire!" he shouted to his men. "We don't shoot women, children, or crackpots." He said to Professor Garet, "All right, mastermind, untie me.

CHAPTER ELEVEN

A submarine surfaced on the Atlantic, far below Superior.

It was obvious to the commander of the submarine, which bore the markings of the Soviet Union, that the runaway town of Superior, being populated entirely by capitalist madmen, was a menace to humanity. The submarine commander made a last-minute check with the radio room, then gave the order to launch the guided missiles which would rid the world of this menace.

The first missile sped skyward.

Superior immediately took evasive action.

First, in its terrific burst of acceleration, everybody was knocked flat.

Next, Superior sped upward for a few hundred feet and everybody was crushed to the ground.

At the same time the first missile, which was now where Superior would have been had it maintained its original course, exploded. A miniature mushroom cloud formed.

The submarine fired again and a second missile streaked up.

Superior dodged again. But this time its direction was down. Everyone who was outdoors—and a few who had been under thin roofs—found himself momentarily suspended in space.

Don and Alis, among the hundreds who had had the ground snatched out from under them, clung to each other and began to fall. All around them were the various adversaries who had been about to clash. Professor Garet had been separated from his machine and they were following separate downward orbits. Many of Thebold's men had dropped their guns but others clung to them, as if it were better to cling to something than merely to fall.

The downward swoop of Superior had taken it out of the immediate path of the second missile, but whoever had changed the townoid's course had apparently failed to take the inhabitants' inertia into immediate consideration. The missile was headed into their midst.

Then two things happened. The missile exploded well away from the falling people. And scores of kangaroo-like Gizls appeared from everywhere and began to snatch people to safety.

Great jumps carried the Gizls into the air and they collected three or four human beings at each leap. The leaps appeared to defy gravity, carrying the creatures hundreds of feet up. The Gizls also appeared to have the faculty of changing course while airborne, saving their charges from other loose objects, but this might have been illusion.

At any rate, Geneva Jervis, who had been hurled up from the roof of Hector's palace, where she had gone in hopes of catching a glimpse of Senator Thebold, was reunited with the Senator when they were rescued by the same Gizl, whose leap had carried him in a great arc virtually from one edge of Superior to the other.

Don Cort, pressed close to Alis and grasped securely against the hairy chest of their particular rescuer, was experiencing a combination of sensations. One, of course, was relief at being snatched from certain death.

Another was the delicious closeness of Alis, who he realized he hadn't been paying enough attention to, in a personal way.

Another was surprise at the number of Gizls who had appeared in the moment of crisis.

Finally he saw beyond doubt that it was the Gizls who were running the entire show—that Hector I, Bobby the Bold, and the pseudo-scientific Garet-Rubach Axis were merely strutters on the stage.

It was the Gizls who were maneuvering Superior as if it were a giant vehicle. It was the Gizls who were exploding the missiles. And it was the alien Gizls who, unlike the would-be belligerents among the Earth-people, were scrupulously saving human lives.

"Thanks," Don said to his rescuing Gizl as it set him and Alis down gently on the hard ground of the golf course.

"Don't mention it," the Gizl said, then leaped off to save others.

"He talked!" Alis said.

Don watched the Gizl make a mid-air grab and haul back a man who had looked as if he might otherwise have gone over the edge. "He certainly did."

"Then that must have been a masquerade, that other time—all that mumbo-jumbo with the Anagrams."

"It must have been, unless they learn awfully fast."

He and Alis clutched each other again as Superior tilted. It remained steady otherwise and they were able to see the ocean, whose surface was marked with splashes as a variety of loose objects fell into it. Don had a glimpse of Professor Garet's machine plummeting down in the midst of most of Superior's vehicular population.

"There's a plane!" Alis cried. "It's going after something on the surface."

"It's the Hustler," Don said. "It's after the submarine."

The B-58's long pod detached itself, became a guided missile and hit the submarine square in the middle. There was a whooshing explosion, the B-58 banked and disappeared from sight under Superior, and the sub went down.

"Sergeant Cort," a voice said, and because Alis was lying with her head on Don's chest she heard it first.

"Is that somebody talking to you, Don? Are you a sergeant?"

"I'm afraid so," he said. "I'll have to explain later. Sergeant Cort here," he said to the Pentagon.

"Things are getting out of hand, Sergeant," the voice of Captain Simmons said.

"Captain, that's the understatement of the week."

"Whatever it is, we can't allow the people of Superior to be endangered any longer."

"No, sir. Is there another submarine?"

"Not as far as we know. I'm talking about the state of anarchy in Superior itself, with each of three factions vying for power. Four, counting the kangaroos."

"They're not kangaroos, sir. They're Gizls."

"Whatever they are. You and I know they're creatures from some other world, and I've managed to persuade the Chief of Staff that this is the case. He's in seeing the Defense Secretary right now. But the State Department isn't buying it."

"You mean they don't believe in the Gizls?"

"They don't believe they're interplanetary. Their whole orientation at State is toward international trouble. Anything interplanetary sends them into a complete flap. We can't even get them to discuss the exploration of the moon, and that's practically around the corner."

"What shall we do, sir?"

"Between you and me, Sergeant—" Captain Simmons' voice interrupted itself. "Never mind that now. Here comes the Defense Secretary."

"Foghorn Frank?" Don asked.

"Shhh."

Frank Fogarty had earned his nickname in his younger years when he commanded a tugboat in New York Harbor. That was before his quick rise in the shipbuilding industry where he got the reputation as a wartime expediter that led to his cabinet appointment.

"Is this the gadget?" Don heard Fogarty say.

"Yes, sir."

"Okay. Sergeant Cort?" Fogarty boomed. "Can you hear me?" It was no wonder they called him Foghorn.

"Yes, sir," Don said, wincing.

"Fine. You've been doing a topnotch job. Don't think I don't know what's been going on. I've heard the tapes. Now, son, are you ready for a little action? We're going to stir them up at State."

"Yes, sir," Don said again.

"Good. Then stand up. No, better not if Superior is still gyrating. Just raise your right hand and I'll give you a field promotion to major. Temporary, of course. I can do that, can't I, General?"

Apparently the Chief of Staff was there, and agreed.

"Right," Fogarty said. "Now, Sergeant, repeat after me…"

Don, too overwhelmed to say anything else, repeated after him.

"Now then, Major Cort, we're going to present the State Department with what they would call a *fait accompli*. You are now Military Governor of Superior, son, with all the power of the U.S. Defense Establishment behind you. A C-97 troop carrier plane is loading. I'll give you the ETA as soon as I know it. A hundred paratroopers. Arrange to meet them at the golf course, near the blimp. And if Senator Thebold tries to interfere—well, handle him tactfully. But I think he'll go along. He's got his headlines and by now he should have been able to find his missing lady friend. Help him in that personal matter if you can. As for Hector Civek and Osbert Garet, be firm. I don't think they'll give you any trouble."

"But, sir," Don said. "Aren't you underestimating the Gizls? If they see paratroops landing they're liable to get unfriendly fast. May I make a suggestion?"

"Shoot, son."

"Well, sir, I think I'd better go try to have a talk with them and see if we can't work something out without a show of force. If you could hold off the troops till I ask for them…"

Foghorn Frank said, "Want to make a deal, eh? If you can do it, fine, but since State isn't willing to admit that there's such a thing as an intelligent kangaroo, alien or otherwise, any little deals you can make with them will have to be unofficial for the time being. All right—I'll hold off on the paratroopers. The important thing is to safeguard the civilian population and uphold the integrity of the United States. You have practically unlimited authority."

"Thank you, Mr. Secretary. I'll do my best."

"Good luck. I'll be listening."

"As I see it," Alis said after Don had explained his connection with the Pentagon, "Senator Thebold licked Hector Civek. Father, who defected from Hector, captured the Senator and vice versa. But now the Gizls have taken over from everybody and you have to fight them—all by your lonesome."

"Not fight them," Don said. "Negotiate with them."

"But the Gizls are on Hector's side. It seems to come full circle. Where do you start?"

Superior had returned to an even keel and Don helped her up. "Let's start by taking a walk over to the bubble gum factory. We'll try to see the Gizl-in-Chief."

There didn't seem to be anyone on the grounds of the McFerson place. The boxcar which had been on the siding near the factory was gone. It was probably at the bottom of the Atlantic by now, along with everything else that hadn't been fastened down. Don wondered if Superior's gyrations had been strong enough to dislodge the train that had originally brought him to town. The Pennsylvania Railroad wouldn't be happy about that.

They saw no one in the mansion and started for the basement room in which they'd had their talk with the Gizl, passing through rooms where the furniture had been knocked about as if by an angry giant. They were stopped en route by Vincent Grande, ex-police chief now Minister of Defense. "All right, kids," he said, "stick 'em up. Your Majesty," he called, "look what I got."

Hector Civek, crownless but still wearing his ermine, came up the stairs. "Put your gun away, Vince. Hello, Alis. Hello, Don. Glad to see you survived the earthquake. I thought we were all headed for kingdom come."

Vincent protested, "This is that traitor Garet's daughter. We can hold her hostage to keep her father in line."

"Nuts," the king said. "I'm getting tired of all this foolishness. I'm sure Osbert Garet is just as shaken up as we are. And that crazy Senator, too. All I want now is for Superior to go back where it came from, as soon as possible. And that's up to Gizl, I'm afraid."

"Have you seen him since the excitement?" Don asked.

"No. He went down that elevator of his when the submarine surfaced. I guess his control room, or whatever it is that makes Superior go, is down there. Let's take a look. Vince, will you put that gun away? Go help them clean up the mess in the kitchen."

Vincent Grande grumbled and went away.

In the basement room, Hector went to the corner and said, "Hey! Anybody down there?"

A deep voice said, "Ascending," and the blue-gray kangaroo-like creature appeared. He stepped off the elevator section. "Greetings, friends."

"Well," Hector said, "I didn't know you could talk."

"Forgive my lack of frankness," Gizl said. "Alis," he said, bowing slightly. "Your Majesty."

"Frankly," Hector said, "I'm thinking of abdicating. I don't think I like being a figurehead. Not when everybody knows about it, anyhow."

"Major Cort," Gizl said.

Don looked startled. "What? How did you know?"

"We have excellent communications. We thank your military for its assistance with the submarine."

"A pleasure. And we thank you and your people for saving us when we went flying."

"Mutuality of effort," Gizl said. "I'll admit a dilemma ensued when the submarine attacked. But our obligation to safeguard human lives outweighed the other alternative— escape to the safety of space. Now suppose we have our conference. You, Major, represent Earth. I, Rezar, represent the survivors of Gorel-zed. Agreed?"

"Rezar?" Don said. "I thought your name was Gizl. And what's Gorel-zed?"

"Little Marie Bendy called me Gizl," Rezar said. "She couldn't pronounce Gorel-zed. I'm afraid I haven't been entirely candid with you about a number of things. But I think I know you better now. I heard your conversation with Foghorn Frank."

Don smiled. "Do you mean you've been listening in ever since I strapped on the transceiver?"

"Oh, yes," Rezar said. "So recapitulation is unnecessary. But we Gizls, so-called, are still a mystery to you, of course. I suppose you'd like some background. Where from, where to, when, and all that."

"I certainly would," Don said. "So would everybody else, I imagine, especially King Hector here, and Mr. Fogarty."

"By all means let us communicate on the highest level," Rezar said. "First, where from, eh?"

"Right. Are you listening, Mr. Secretary?"

"I sure am," Fogarty said. "What's more, son, you're being piped directly into the White House—and a few other places."

"Good," Rezar said. "Now marvel at our saga."

CHAPTER TWELVE

The end of a civilization is a tragic thing.

On the desert planet of Gorel-zed, the last world to survive the slow nova of its sun, the Gizls, once the pests but now through brain surgery the possessors in their hardy bodies of the accumulated knowledge of the frail human beings, were preparing to flee. Their self-supporting ships were ready, capable of crossing space to the ends of the universe.

But their universe was barren. No planet could receive them. All were doomed as was theirs, Gorel-zed. They set out for a new galaxy, knowing they would not reach it but that their descendants might. They became nomads of space, self-sufficient.

For generations they wandered, their population diminishing. Their scientist-philosophers evolved the theory that accounted for their spaceborn ennui with life, their acceptance of their fate, their eventual doom. They had no roots, no place of their own. They had only the mechanistic world of their ships—which were vehicles, not a land. They must find a home of their own, or die.

Several times in their odyssey they had come to a planet which could have housed them. But each time an injunction which had been built into them at the time of the brain surgery prevented them from staying. The doomed human beings on Gorel-zed had built into the very fiber of the Gizls—who were, after all, only animals—the injunction that no human being could be harmed for their comfort.

This meant that the world of Ladnora, whose gentle saffron inhabitants were incapable of offering resistance, could not be conquered. The Ladnorans, in their generosity, had offered the refugees from Gorel-zed a hemisphere of their own. But the Gizls required a world of their own, not a half-world. They accepted a small continent only and made it spaceborne and took it with them.

The Crevisians were the next to be visited. They ruled a belt of fertile land around the equator of their world—the rest was icy waste. The Gizls took a slice of each polar region and, joining them, made them spaceborne.

In time they reached the system of Sol.

Mars attracted them first because of its sands. Mars was like Gorel-zed in many ways. But that very resemblance meant it was not for them. Mars was a dead world, as their own Gorel-zed had become.

But the next planet they came to was a green planet. The Gizls moored the acquisitions in the asteroid belt and visited Earth.

Here, at their planetfall, Australia, was the perfect land. Even its inhabitants—the great kangaroos, the smaller wallabies—breathed Home to the Gizls. But there were also the human beings who had made the land their own. And though memory of their origin had weakened in the Gizls, the injunction had not.

For a time they set up a kind of camp in the great central desert and with delight found their legs again. Out of the cramped ships they came, to bound in freedom and fresh breathable air across the wasteland. But hardy, naked, black human beings lived in the desert and they attacked the Gizls with their primitive weapons. And when the Gizls fled, not wishing to harm them, they came to white men, who attacked them with explosive weapons.

And so they took to their ships and were spaceborne again. But the attraction of Earth was strong and they sought another continent, called North America.

And in the center of it they found a great race whose technology was nearly as great as their own. These people had an intelligence and drive which rivaled that of their human antecedents, whose minds had been transferred to the Gizl's hardy, cumbersome bodies.

Rezar paused. His intelligent eyes seemed misplaced in his heavy animal body.

"What attracted you to Superior, of all places?" Alis asked.

Rezar seemed to smile. "Two things. Cavalier and bubble gum."

"What?" Alis said. "You're kidding!"

"No," Rezar said. "It's true. Bubble gum because after generations of subsistence on capsule food our teeth had weakened and loosened, and bubble gum strengthened them. Nourishment, no. Exercise, yes. And Cavalier Institute because here were men who spoke in terms which paralleled the secret of our spacedrive."

Alis laughed. "This would make Father expire of joy," she said. "But now you know he's just a phony."

"Alas," Rezar said. "Yes, alas. But he was so close. Magnology. Cosmolineation. It's jargon merely, as we learned in time. Osbert Garet is mad. Harmless, but mad."

Don asked Rezar, "But if this built-in morality of yours is so strong, why didn't it prevent you from taking off with Superior?"

Rezar replied, "There are factions among us now. An evolution of a sort, I suppose. Nothing is static. One faction..." He tapped his chest. "...is completely bound by the injunction. But in the other, self-preservation places a limit on the injunction."

The explanation seemed to be that the other faction, which grew in strength with every failure to find a world of their own, felt that on a planet such as Earth, with a history of men warring against men, required the Gizls to be no more moral than the human inhabitants themselves.

"The Good Gizls versus the Bad Gizls?" Alis asked.

Rezar seemed to smile. The Bad Gizls, led by one called Kaliz, had got the upper hand for a time and elevated Superior, intending to join it to the bits and pieces of other planets they had previously collected and stored in the asteroid belt. But Rezar's influence had persuaded them not to head directly into space—at least not until they had solved the problem of how to put Superior's inhabitants "ashore" first.

Don, unaccustomed to his new role of interplanetary arbitrator, said tentatively:

"I can't authorize you to take Superior, even if you do put us all ashore, but there must be a comparable piece of Earth we could let you have."

"But Superior is not all," Rezar said. "To use one of your nautical expressions, Superior merely represents a shake-down cruise. Our ability to detach such a populated center had shown the feasibility of raising other typical communities—such as New York, Magnitogorsk and Heidelberg—each a different example of Earth culture."

Don heard a gasp from the Pentagon—or it might have come from the White House.

"You mean you've burrowed under each one of those 'communities'?" Don asked.

Rezar shrugged. "Kaliz's faction," he said, as if to dissociate himself from the project of removing some of Earth's choicest property. "They aim at a history-museum of habitable worlds."

"Interplanetary souvenirs," Alis said. "With quick-frozen inhabitants? Don, what are you going to do?"

Don didn't even know what to say. His eyes met Hector's.

"Don't look at me," Hector said. "I definitely abdicate."

"Look," Don said to Rezar, "how far advanced are these plans? I mean, is there a deadline for this mass levitation?"

"Twenty-four hours, your time," Rezar said.

"Can't you stop them? Aren't you the boss?"

The alien turned Don's question back on him. "Are *you* the boss?"

Don had started to shake his head when Foghorn Frank's voice boomed out.

"Yes, by thunder, he *is* the boss! Don, raise your right hand. I'm going to make you a brigadier general. No, blast it, a full general. Repeat after me…"

General Don Cort squared his shoulders. He was almost getting used to these spot promotions.

"Now negotiate," Fogarty said. "You hear me, Mr. Gizl-Rezar? The United States of America stands behind General Cort." There was no audible objection from the White House. "Who stands behind you?"

"A democratic government," Rezar said. "Like yours."

"You represent them?" Fogarty asked.

"With my council, yes."

"Then we can make a deal. Talk to him, Don. I'll shut up now."

Don said to Rezar, "Was it your decision to burrow under New York and Magnitogorsk and Heidelberg?"

"I agreed to it, finally."

"But you agreed to it in the belief that the Earth-people were a warring people and that your old prohibitions did not apply. But we are not a warring people. Earth is at peace."

"Is it?" Rezar asked sadly. "Your plane warred on the submarine."

"In self-defense," Don said. "Don't forget that we defended you, too. And we'd do it again—but not unless provoked."

Rezar looked thoughtful. He tapped his long fingernails on the table. Finally he said, "I believe you. But I must talk to my people first, as you have talked to yours. Let us meet later..." He seemed to be making a mental calculation. "...in three hours. Where? Here?"

"How about Cavalier?" Alis suggested. "It would be the first important thing that ever happened there."

For the first time since Superior took off, all of the town's elected or self-designated representatives met amicably. They gathered in the common room at Cavalier Institute as they waited for Rezar and his council to arrive for the talks which could decide, not only the fate of Superior, but of New York and two foreign cities as well.

Apparently the Pentagon expected Don to pretend he had authority to speak for Russia and Germany as well as the United States. But could he speak for the United States constitutionally? He was sure that Bobby Thebold, comprising exactly one percent of that great deliberative body, the Senate, would let him know if he went too far, crisis or no crisis.

The Senator, reunited with Geneva Jervis, sat holding her hand on a sofa in front of the fireplace in which logs blazed cheerfully. Thebold looked untypically placid. Jen Jervis, completely sober and with her hair freshly reddened, had greeted Don with a cool nod.

Thebold had been chagrined at learning that Don Cort was not the yokel he had taken him for. But he recovered quickly, saying that if there was any one thing he had learned in his Senate career it was the art of compromise. He would go along with the duly authorized representative of the Pentagon, with which he had always had the most cordial of relations.

"Isn't that so, sweetest of all the pies?" he said to Jen Jervis.

Jen looked uncomfortable. "Please, Bobby," she said. "Not in public." The Senator squeezed her hand.

Professor Garet, whose wife and daughter were serving tea, stood with Ed Clark near the big bay window, through which they looked occasionally to see if the Gizls were coming. Maynard Rubach sat in a leather armchair next to Hector Civek, who had discarded his ermine and wore an old heavy tweed suit. Doc Bendy sat off in a corner by himself. He was untypically quiet.

Don Cort, despite his four phantom stars, was telling himself he must not let these middle-aged men make him feel like a boy. Each of them had had a chance to do something positive and each had failed.

"Gentlemen," Don said, "my latest information from Washington confirms that the Gizls have actually tunneled under the cities they say their militant faction wants to take up to the asteroid belt, just as they dug in under Superior before it took off. So they're not bluffing."

"How'd we find out about Magnitogorsk?" Ed Clark asked. "Iron curtain getting rusty?"

Don told him that the Russians, impressed by the urgency of an unprecedented telephone call from the White House to the Kremlin, had finally admitted that their great industrial city was sitting on top of a honeycomb. The telephone conversation had also touched delicately on the subject of the submarine that had been sunk in mid-Atlantic, and there had been tacit agreement that the sub commander had exceeded his authority in firing the missiles and that the sinking would not be referred to again.

Maynard Rubach turned away from the window. "Here they come. Three of them. But they're not coming from the direction of the McFerson place."

"They could have come up from under the grandstand." Don said. "Miss Jervis and I found one of their tunnels there. Remember, Jen?"

Jen Jervis colored slightly and Don was sorry he'd brought it up. "Yes," she said. "I fainted and Don—Mr. Cort— General Cort—helped me."

"I'm obliged to the general," Senator Thebold said.

Professor Garet went to the door. The three Gizls followed him into the room. Everyone stood up formally. There was some embarrassed scurrying around because no one had remembered that the Gizls required backless chairs to accommodate their tails.

The Gizls, looking remarkably alike, sat close together. Don tentatively addressed the one in the middle.

"Gentlemen," he said, "first it is my privilege to award to you in the name of the President, the Medal of Merit in appreciation of your quick action in saving uncounted lives during the submarine incident. The actual medal will be presented to you when we re-establish physical contact with Earth."

Rezar, who, it turned out, was the one in the middle, accepted with a grave bow. "Our regret is that we were unable to prevent the loss of many valuable objects as well," he said.

"Mr. Rezar," Don said, "I haven't been trained in diplomacy so I'll speak plainly. We don't intend to give up New York. Contrary to general belief, there are about eight million people who *do* want to live there. And I'm sure the inhabitants of Heidelberg and Magnitogorsk feel the same way about their cities."

"Then you yield Superior," Rezar said.

"I didn't say that."

"Yield Superior and we will guarantee safe passage to Earth for all its inhabitants. We only want its physical facilities."

"We'll yield the bubble gum factory to help your dental problem—for suitable reparations," Don said.

"Payment will be made for anything we take. Give us Superior intact, including the factory and Cavalier Institute, and we will transport to any place you name an area of equal size from the planet Mars."

"Mars?" Don said. "That'd be a very valuable piece of real estate for the researchers."

"Take it," Don heard Frank Fogarty say from the Pentagon.

Professor Garet spoke up. "If Cavalier goes, I go with it. I won't leave it."

"And I won't leave you, Osbert," his wife said. "Will there be air up there among the asteroids?"

"We are air-breathers like you," Rezar said. "When we have assembled our planet there will be plenty. You will be welcome, Professor and Mrs. Garet."

"Hector?" Don said. "You're still mayor of Cavalier. What do you think?"

"They can have it," Hector said. "I'll take a nice steady civil service job with the Federal Government, if you can arrange it."

"Hector," Ed Clark said, "I think that sums up why you've never been a howling success in politics. You don't give a damn for the people. All you care about is yourself."

Hector shrugged. "You needn't be so holy-sounding, Eddie-boy," he said. "Why isn't the *Sentry* out this week? I'll tell you why. Because you've been so busy filing to the Trimble-Grayson papers on Thebold's private radio that you haven't had time for anything else. How much are they paying you?"

Ed Clark, deflated, muttered, "News is news."

"Is that what you were doing in Senator Thebold's Gripe Room on the midway?" Don asked Clark. "Making this deal?"

"Now, General," Thebold said. "Would you deprive the people of their right to know? Throughout my Senate career I have carried the torch against government censorship, which is the path to a totalitarian state."

"I'm sure part of the deal was that Clark's copy didn't make you anything less than a hero," Don said.

"Don't be too righteous, young man," Thebold said. "'Lest ye be judged,' as they say. Are you not at this moment bargaining away a piece of a sovereign State of the sovereign United States? I don't happen to represent Ohio, but if I did I would rise in the upper chamber to demand your court-martial."

"At ease, Senator!" Don ordered. "You're not in the upper chamber now. You're on an artificial satellite which at any moment is apt to take off into outer space."

Doc Bendy spoke for the first time: "Oops-a-daisy! You tell 'im, Donny-boy. Soo-perior—the town everybody looks up to."

Don frowned at him. Bendy had sunk deep into his chair in his corner. He acknowledged Don's look with a broad smile that vanished in a hiccup.

"Y' don't have to say it, Donny. I been drinkin'. Ever since Superior looped the looperior and flung me feet over forehead into the bee-yond. Shatterin' experience to have nothin' but a kangaroo-hop between you and eternity. Yop, ol' Bendy's been on a bender ever since. But you carry on, boy. Y' doin' a great job."

"Thanks," Don said in irony. "I guess that completes the roster of those qualified to speak for Superior. Oh, I'm sorry, Dr. Rubach. Did you have something to say?"

But all the portly president of Cavalier had to say, though he said it at great length, was that if Cavalier were taken as part of a package deal, its trustees would have to receive adequate compensation. Professor Garet tugged at his sleeve and said, "Sit down, Maynard. They've already said they'll pay."

Fogarty's voice rumbled at Don: "Let's try to speed things up, General. Close the deal on Superior, at least, before the press get there."

"The press?"

"The rest of the papers couldn't let the Trimble-Grayson chain keep their exclusive. Clark's going to have lots of company soon. The boys have hired a vertiplane. First one off the assembly line. You've seen it. Lands anywhere."

"Okay, I'll try to hurry it up." To the Gizls Don said, "All right. You take Superior, minus its people, and bring us a piece of Mars."

"Agreed," Rezar said. It was as easy as that. Nobody objected. Too many of Superior's self-proclaimed saviors had been caught with their motives showing.

"You've got to give up New York, though," Don said. He felt as if he were playing a game of interplanetary Monopoly. "We'll give you a chunk of the great central desert instead, if Australia's willing. (Would that come under the South East Asia Treaty Organization, Mr. Secretary?) Complete with kangaroos and assorted wallabies, if you want them."

"Agreed," said Rezar.

Don sighed quietly to himself. It should be smooth sailing now that the hurdle of New York was past.

But Kaliz, the one Alis had called the Bad Gizl, shook his head violently and spoke for the first time. "No," he said firmly. "We must have New York. It is by far the greatest of our conquests and I will not yield it."

Rezar said sharply, "We have foresworn conquest."

"I am tired of your moralizing," Kaliz said. "We are dealing with beings whose greatest respect is for power. If we temporize now we will lose their respect. They will think our new world weak and itself open to conquest. We have the power—let us use it. I say take New York *and* its people and hold them hostage. The city is ready for lifting."

"No!" Don said. "You can't have New York."

Kaliz seemed to smile. "We already have it. It's merely a question of transporting it." He put a long-fingered hand to his furry chest where, almost hidden in the blue-gray fur, was a flat perforated disk. He said into it, "Show them that New York is ours!"

"Wait!" Rezar said.

"Merely a demonstration," Kaliz told him, "for the moment at least."

Frank Fogarty's voice, alarmed, said urgently, "Tell him we believe him. New York's reporting an earthquake, or something very like it. For God's sake tell him to put it back while we reorient our thinking."

Kaliz nodded in satisfaction. "The city is as it was. Our people under New York raised it a mere fraction of an inch. It could as easily have been a mile. Do not underestimate our power."

Rezar was agitated. "We came in peace," he said to his fellow Gizl. "Let us not leave in war. There's power on both sides, capable of untold destruction. Neither must use it. We are a democratic people. Let us vote. I say we must not take New York."

"And I say we must," Kaliz told him, "in self-interest."

They turned to the third of their people, who had been looking from one to the other, his eyes reflecting indecision.

Kaliz barked at him: "Well, Ezial? Vote!"

Ezial said, "I abstain."

Deadlock.

Don was sweating. He looked at the others in the room. They were tense but silent, apparently willing to leave it up to Don and his link with the Defense Department.

Frank Fogarty's voice said:

"SAC has been airborne in total strength for half an hour, General. It was a purely precautionary alert at the time."

Don started to interrupt.

"I know they hear me," the Secretary of Defense said. "I intend that they should. We don't want to fight but we will if we must. Son..." The rough voice faltered for a moment. "If necessary, we'll destroy Superior to kill this alien and save New York. As a soldier, I hope you understand. It's the lives of three thousand people against the lives of eight million."

Only Don and the Gizl had heard. Don looked across the room and into Alis' eyes. She gave him a tentative smile, noting his grave expression.

"Yes, sir," Don said finally.

Rezar spoke. "This is folly." He touched the disk in the fur of his own chest.

"No!" Kaliz cried.

"It is time," Rezar said. "We are beginning to fail in our mission." He spoke reverently into the disk, "My lord, awake."

Kaliz said quickly, "Raise New York! Take it up!"

"They will not obey you now," Rezar said. "I have invoked the counsel of the Master."

The man was frail and incredibly old. He had sparse white hair and a deeply lined face, but his eyes were alert and wise.

He wore a cloak-like garment of soft, warm-looking material. His expression was one of kindliness but strength.

The doorbell had rung and Mrs. Garet had answered it. The old man had walked slowly into the room, followed respectfully by two Gizls.

"My lord," said Rezar. He got to his feet and bowed, as did the other Gizls. "I had hoped to let you sleep until your new world had been prepared for you. But the risk was great that, if I delayed, your world would never be. Forgive me."

"You did well," the old man said.

Don stood up too, feeling the sense of awe that this personage inspired. "How do you do, sir," he said.

"How do you do, General Cort."

"You know my name?"

"I know many things. Too many for such a frail old body. But someone had to preserve the heritage of our people, and I was chosen."

"Won't you sit down, sir?"

"I'll stand, thanks. I've rested long enough. Generations, as a matter of fact. Shall I answer some of your obvious questions? I'd better say a few things quickly, before Foghorn Frank hits the panic button."

Don smiled. "Can he hear you or shall I repeat everything?"

"Oh, he hears me. I've got gadgets galore, even though I'm between planets at the moment. I must say it's a pleasure to be among people again." He nodded pleasantly around the room.

Mrs. Garet smiled to him. "Would you like a cup of tea?"

"Later, perhaps, thank you. First I must assure you and everyone of Earth that no one will be harmed by us and that we want nothing for our new world that you are not willing to give."

"That's good to hear," Don said. "I gather you've been in some kind of suspended animation since you left your old world. So I wonder how you're able to speak English."

"Everything was suspended but the subconscious. That kept perking along, absorbing everything the Gizls fed into it. And they've been absorbing your culture for ten years, so I'm pretty fluent. And I certainly know enough to apologize for all the inconvenience my associates have caused you in their zeal to re-establish the human race of Gorel-zed. In the case of Kaliz, of course, it was excessive zeal which will necessitate his rehabilitation."

"Your pardon, Master," Kaliz said humbly.

"Granted. But you'll be rehabilitated anyway."

Don asked, "Did I understand you to say you plan to re-establish your race? Do you mean there are more of you, aside from the kangaroo-people?"

"Oh, yes. Young people. The youngest of all from Gorel-zed. They were put to sleep like me, to be ready to carry on when their new world is built. I won't wake them till then. I hope to live that much longer."

"I'm sure you will, sir."

"Kind of you. But let's get on with the horse trading. Of course we won't take New York, or the two other cities." (There was a collection of sighs of relief from Washington.) "But we would like some of your uninhabited jungle land—the lusher the better, to help us out in the oxygen department. We'd also like some of your air, if you can spare it. We've got a planet to supply now, not just ships."

"How would you get air across space?" Don asked.

"At the moment," the Master said, "I'm afraid we're not prepared to barter our scientific knowledge."

"I didn't mean to pry. It just didn't seem to be something you could do. Do you think we could spare some air, Mr. Secretary?"

"I'll have to ask the science boys about that one," Frank Fogarty said. "Meanwhile it's okay with Australia on the desert. But your Gizl friends have to agree to relocate the aborigines from that tract, and they must take every last rabbit or it's no deal."

"Agreed," the Master said with a smile. "But please ask their stockmen to hold their fire. My friends only *look* like kangaroos."

As Don and the Master were making arrangements for Superior to touch down so its people could be transferred to Earth, a blaze of light stabbed down from the sky. Through the window they saw the vertiplane settling slowly to the campus.

"It sure beats a blimp," Senator Thebold said in admiration.

Professor Garet got up to look. "It's the press," he said to his wife. "You might as well invite them in. I hope we have enough tea."

The vertiplane's door opened and the first wave of reporters spilled out.

CHAPTER THIRTEEN

As Superior headed back across the Atlantic, the Earth-people were given a farewell tour. For the first time they had an authorized look at the underground domain of the Gizls, which they reached through the tunnel that led below from under Cavalier's grandstand.

The observation room which Don and Jen Jervis had found was connected by a hidden elevator to a vast main chamber. A control console formed the entire wall of one end of it. Half a dozen Gizls stood at the base of the console. From time to time one of them would launch himself upward with his powerful legs, grab a protruding rung, make an adjustment, then drop lightly back to the floor.

Don and Alis stood for a moment watching Professor Garet, who was tugging at his beard as he became aware of the magnitude of the operation which drove Superior through the skies and was soon to take it across space to the asteroid belt.

"Poor Father," Alis whispered to Don. "Magnology in action, after all these years—and he didn't have a thing to do with it."

"Is that why he wants to go with the Master?"

"I imagine so. If he stayed on Earth he'd have nothing. He's too old to start again. It's kind of them to take him—and Mother. In a way, I suppose, his going is justification for his years of work. He'll at least be close to the things he might have developed in the right circumstances."

"He certainly won't be lonely," Don said. "Have you noticed the rush to emigrate? Cheeky McFerson's decided to stick with his bubble gum factory. He says the Gizls are a ready-made market. He saw one of them cram five Super-Bubs into his mouth, at one time. That's twenty-five cents right there."

Alis giggled. "And half of the student body of Cavalier wants to go. You'd think they'd be disillusioned with Father, but they're not. I guess they had to be crazy to enroll in the first place."

"Senator Thebold's started campaigning to be named U.S. Ambassador to Superior. I heard him talking to the man from the *New York Times*. I suspect they'll give it to him— they'll need his influence to get Senate approval of the treaty with the Gizls."

"I had a little talk with Jen Jervis," Alis said. "She's radiant, have you noticed? The Senator finally asked her to marry him. That's all that was the matter with her—Bobby the Bold had left her hanging by her thumbs too long."

"I guess he did." Don sought a way to get the conversation away from Jen Jervis. "Where's Doc Bendy? He certainly turned out to be a disappointment."

"Poor Doc!" Alis said. "He's always the first to form a committee. But then his enthusiasm wears off and he goes back to the bottle. Only now he's got a keg."

Don snapped his fingers. "The keg. I almost forgot about that matter duplicator. If it can give you perfume and Doc rum... Come on. Let's reopen negotiations with the Master."

They found the old man surrounded by a group of reporters, being charmingly evasive with the science editor of *Time*. Professor Garet had now joined this group, where he listened as eagerly as a student.

The Master was showing the vault-like chamber in which he had spent the generations since the spaceships left Gorelzed. He let them examine the coffin-sized drawer that had been his bed and indicated the others where the younger ones still slept, awaiting the birth of their new planet. Don counted fewer than three dozen drawers.

"Is that all?" he asked.

"Infants and children take up less room," the Master said. "There are two or three in each drawer, and still others in the ships that never come to Earth. Even so, we number fewer than a thousand."

"But you have the matter duplicator," Don said. "Won't it work on people?"

"Unfortunately, no. Transubstantiation has never worked on living cells. Don't think we haven't tried. We shall have to encourage early marriages and hope for a high birth rate."

"Now about this transubstantiator," the *Time* man said, and Garet's head cocked in delight, apparently at the resounding sound of the word. "What's the principle? You don't have to give away the secret—just give me a general idea."

The Master shook his head.

Don asked, "What will you trade for the transubstantiator and the paralysis scepter you gave Hector?"

The old man smiled. "Not even New York," he said. "Our moral code couldn't permit us to trade either. Earth has enough problems already."

"Offer him the formula for fusion," Frank Fogarty's voice said from the Pentagon.

The old man shuddered. "I heard that," he said. "No, thank you, Mr. Secretary!"

"This is the *clean* bomb," Fogarty said. "It ought to come in very handy in construction work on your new planet."

"We will try to manage in our own way," the Master said. He asked Garet, "Wouldn't you say that magnology was sufficient for our purposes, Professor?"

Alis' father beamed at being consulted and hearing his own term applied to the Gorel-zed propulsion system.

"More than sufficient," he said enthusiastically. "Preferable, in fact. Magnology is safe, stressless, and permanently powerful in stasis. It is the ultimate in gravity-beam nullification. If anything can glue the asteroids back into the planet they once were, magnology will do it. You can understand how I was misled. Your system so fitted my theory that I imagined it was I who had caused Superior to rise from Earth."

"I understand perfectly," the Master replied graciously. "And I cannot say how glad I am that you and Mrs. Garet have chosen to stay with Cavalier and Superior and become citizens of our new world."

"What will you call your new planet?" the AP man asked. "Asteroida? Something like that?"

"We haven't decided. I welcome suggestions."

The UPI man was inspired. "How about Neworld?" he asked. "That describes it perfectly, doesn't it? New world—Neworld?" He wrote it on a piece of paper and admired it.

"Thank you," the Master said. "Well certainly consider it."

The UPI man was satisfied. He had a lead for his story.

SUPERIOR, Nov. 6 (AP)—The floating city of Superior, Earthbound again after nearly six days of aerial meandering, prepared today to discharge its former residents. Its new inhabitants, the kangaroo-like Gizls who came from beyond the stars to swing an unprecedented barter deal involving the United States, Russia and Germany, said they would leave almost immediately to join Superior with the new planet they have been building in the asteroid belt between Mars and Jupiter...

HEIDELBERG, Nov. 6 (AP)—This university city said good-by today to some 400 interplanetary visitors it belatedly realized had long been burrowed under it. The first officially acknowledged flying saucer landed on Heidelberg's outskirts early today and took aboard the

Gizls, who, but for the shrewd maneuvering of the U. S. Secretary of State, "Foghorn Frank" Fogarty, acting through a hastily commissioned ex-sergeant troubleshooter, General Don Cort...

MOSCOW, November 6 (Reuters)—The industrial city of Magnitogorsk was assured of remaining Soviet territory today with the departure of 1,000 kangaroo-like aliens. These visitors from Gorel-zed, the doomed world whose survivors will increase the number of planets in the solar system to ten with the creation between Mars and Jupiter of...

From the editorial page of the New York Daily News:
Nice Knowing You, Gizls, But—
Next time you visit us, how about doing it openly, instead of burrowing underground like a bunch of Reds?

Bulletin
ABOARD THE SPACESHIP SUPERIOR, Nov. 6 (UPI)—This former Ohio town, adapted for space travel, took off for the asteroid belt today after transferring 2,878 of its citizens to a convoy of buses bound for a relocation center. The other 122 of its previous population of 3,000 chose to remain aboard to pioneer the birth of the tenth planet of the solar system—Neworld.

Neworld, named by the United Press International correspondent accompanying the survivors of the burned-out planet of Gorel-zed, will become the second known inhabited planet in the solar system...

"Just a minute, Alis," Don said.

"No, sir, Sergeant-General Donald Cort, sir. Not a minute longer. You tell him now."

"All right. Sir," Don Cort (Gen., temp.) said to Frank Fogarty, Secretary of Defense, "has the mission been accomplished?"

Don and Alis were in the back seat of an army staff car that was leading the bus convoy.

"Looks that way, son. Our best telescopes can't see them any more. I'd say Neworld was well on its way to a-borning."

Alis Garet, her arms around Don and her head on his shoulder, spoke directly into the transceiver. "Mr. Fogarty, are you aware that I haven't had a single minute alone with this human radio station since I've know him? This is the most inhibited man in the entire U. S. Army."

"Miss Garet," the Defense Secretary said, "I understand perfectly. When I was courting Mrs. Fogarty I was a pilot on the Meseck Line... Well, never mind that. Mission accomplished, General Cort, my boy."

"Then, sir," Don said, "Sergeant Cort respectfully requests permission to disconnect this blasted invasion of privacy so he can ask Miss Alis Garet if she thinks two of us can live on a non-com's pay."

The driver of the staff car, a sergeant himself, said over his shoulder, "Can't be done, General."

Fogarty said, "Don't be too anxious to revert to the ranks, my boy. I'll admit the T/O for generals isn't wide open but I'm sure we can compromise somewhere between three stripes and four stars. Suppose you take a ten-day delay en route to Washington while we see what we can do. I'll meet you in the White House on November sixteenth. The President tells me he wants to pin a medal on you."

"Yes, sir," Don said. Alis was very close and he was only half listening. "Any further orders, sir?"

"Just one, Don. Kiss her for me, too. Over to you."

"Yes, sir!" Don said. "Over and out."

THE END

If you've enjoyed this book, you will not want to miss these terrific titles...

ARMCHAIR SCI-FI & HORROR DOUBLE NOVELS, $12.95 each

D-91   **THE TIME TRAP** by Henry Kuttner
       THE LUNAR LICHEN by Hal Clement

D-92   **SARGASSO OF LOST STARSHIPS** by Poul Anderson
       THE ICE QUEEN by Don Wilcox

D-93   **THE PRINCE OF SPACE** by Jack Williamson
       POWER by Harl Vincent

D-94   **PLANET OF NO RETURN** by Howard Browne
       THE ANNIHILATOR COMES by Ed Earl Repp

D-95   **THE SINISTER INVASION** by Edmond Hamilton
       OPERATION TERROR by Murray Leinster

D-96   **THE WORLD-MOVER** by George O. Smith
       TRANSIENT by Ward Moore

D-97   **FORTY DAYS HAS SEPTEMBER** by Milton Lesser
       THE DEVIL'S PLANET by David Wright O'Brien

D-98   **THE CYBERENE** by Rog Phillips
       BADGE OF INFAMY by Lester del Rey

D-99   **THE VENGEANCE OF MARTIN BRAND** by Raymond A. Palmer
       THE JUSTICE OF MARTIN BRAND by Raymond A. Palmer

D-100   **WIDE-OPEN PLANET** by L. Sprague de Camp
       AND THEN THE TOWN TOOK OFF by Richard Wilson

ARMCHAIR SCIENCE FICTION CLASSICS, $12.95 each

C-31   **THE GOLDEN GUARDSMEN**
       by S. J. Byrne

C-32   **ONE AGAINST THE MOON**
       by Donald A. Wollheim

C-33   **HIDDEN CITY**
       by Chester S. Geier

ARMCHAIR SCIENCE FICTION & HORROR GEMS SERIES, $12.95 each

G-9   **SCIENCE FICTION GEMS, Vol. Five**
       Clifford D. Simak and others

G-10   **HORROR GEMS, Vol. Five**
       E. Hoffman Price and others